A B S E N C E

Translation copyright © 1990 by Farrar, Straus and Giroux, Inc.

All rights reserved

Originally published in German under the title Die Abwesenheit,
© Suhrkamp Verlag, Frankfurt am Main, 1987

Published simultaneously in Canada by Harper & Collins, Toronto

Printed in the United States of America

Designed by Cynthia Krupat

First edition, 1990

Library of Congress Cataloging-in-Publication Data

Handke, Peter.

[Abwesenheit. English]

Absence / Peter Handke; translated by Ralph Manheim.—1st ed.

Translation of: Die Abwesenheit.

I. Title.

PT2668.A5A6413   1990   833'.914—dc20   89-77504

Portions of this book were previously published
in Antaeus and Fiction

A horse of the kingdom—his qualities are complete. Now he looks anxious, now to be losing the way, now to be forgetting himself. Such a horse prances along, or pushes on, spurning the dust and now knowing where he is.

CHUANG TZU

Also by Peter Handke

A B S E N C E

Late one Sunday afternoon the statues on the city squares are casting long shadows and the humped asphalt of the deserted suburban streets is giving off a bronze glow. The only sounds from inside the café are the hum of the ventilator and an intermittent clatter. A glance goes up to the branches of a plane tree, as if someone were standing under it, watching the countless incessantly swinging seedpods, the large-lobed, long-stemmed leaves, which move spasmodically, all together, like a semaphore, and the swaying, deep-yellow nests of sunlight in the foliage; where the blotchy trunk forks there is a hollow that might be the home of some animal. Another glance goes down to a fast-flowing river, which, as seen from the bank, the sun shines through to the bottom, revealing a long fish, light-gray like the pebbles rolling in the current below it. At the same time, the rays of the sun reach the wall of a basement room, filling the entire pictureless surface and giving the whitewash a grainy look. The room is neither abandoned nor uninhabited; it is populated, always at eye level, by the silhouettes of flying birds and, at intervals, of passersby on the road, for the most part bicyclists. Likewise, at eye level, a lone Far Eastern mountain appears on the horizon, lit by the last rays of the sun. The picture comes closer, bringing into prominence at its rounded upper edge the precipitous summit which, with its crags and chimneys, ledges and glassy walls, suggests an impregnable and inaccessible castle. The sun has set; here and there a light in a house; on the blank wall of the basement room the reflection of the yellow sky is traversed by patterns that have now lost their outlines. The wall is now so totally blank that the deep-red number on a small tear-off calendar moves into the picture.

In a park there is a castle-like nineteenth-century building with tall windows surmounted by triangular tympana and just under the eaves some hundred attic windows running all around the building. The immensity of this edifice makes the park seem small; vegetation, walks, and benches are unimpressive; only an aborted avenue of birches and the solitary plane tree with its pillar-like branches, which seems to grow out of an enormous bench, give an intimation of a past epoch. Because it is Sunday afternoon, the expressways on either side of the apparent castle are not being used by trucks but only by private cars. Unlike the few houses scattered roundabout, which in the presence of the huge building look like little more than huts, the castle shows light in almost all its windows, as though some great festivity were in progress from floor to floor and, through the open double doors, from hall to hall. But the building is an old people's home or, as the sign at the entrance indicates, a SANATORIUM FOR THE ELDERLY, and the bright serried window squares signify separate rooms. In some of them, behind often curtainless panes, the silhouettes of the occupants, always immobile, inactive, and for the most part unseeing. Other windows are open, making the rooms look deserted in spite of the burning ceiling lights, the potted plants, and the birdcages. Even the lights from the television sets leap across empty walls and change color for no one but themselves. The clicking of an electric iron and the clatter when it is set down come from a room occupied by one of the staff. The head in the attic window, with the all-

seeing eyes of a detective or a scientist, is that of a young
man, not an inmate of the home. The only laughter in the
festively illumined transept is that of the audience on the
television screen, which erupts at regular intervals, as
though on command. The only natural singing comes from
a kitchen maid who is lifting the lid from an enormous tin
pot in the white-tiled basement; actually, it is more like
short snatches of monotone humming, with which she is
merely testing her voice. The gravel path to the entrance
ends at a low step, an impediment large enough that it has
to be flanked on either side by a railing, whose brass sup-
ports, along with the elbow crutches of the one elderly
person still to be seen there, are the only glittering spots
under the yellow sky.

At the back of one of the few apparently unlit rooms,
a lamp is burning after all; it is mounted on a lectern. In
the surrounding half darkness, this lamp, tiny as it is, casts
a bright circle of light on the lectern, on which lies an open
notebook, with outsized hard covers, wrapped in cracked,
many-times-mended canvas, its paper spotted with mold,
as though the whole had a story of its own, as though it
had often been exposed to sun and rain, or had even been
part of someone's luggage on the high seas. The pages are
covered with columns of signs that vaguely suggest hiero-
glyphics. Beside them, written in a clear, official-looking,
yet childlike hand, are words that seem to be attempts (some
followed by question marks) to decipher the signs, such as
"to bear in mind"; "to master"; "to break camp"; "to set
out"; "to sit down?"; "the runnel?"; "the cliff on the border?"; "the watershed?" In the space under the spine of the
notebook: a black hexagonal pencil. The near-emptiness of

the room, with its long, broad floorboards, whose converging lines, marked by spiral knotholes and polished nail-
heads, tend toward a single point in the distance, makes it
seem spacious, while the oval ornaments of its stucco ceiling
give it an air of nobility. The lectern stands on a raised
platform, suggesting the balcony in the study of a medieval
scholar. The only other furniture is a folding bed in a wall
niche, stored there, one supposes, in anticipation of some
expedition; in lieu of a blanket a sleeping bag is draped over
the naked frame. The slight rounding at the top of the
window makes it look like an arcade. On the floor below
it two dumbbells, their paint flaking, and an empty, shapeless, and shrunken knapsack.

The occupant, who is standing at the window, is not
an inmate of the home; he is the master of this room. True,
he is holding a stick, but it is not a crutch—it is a walking
stick, made of hard, rigid, almost unbreakable rosewood;
with the few large, sharp-beaked thorns that are still on it,
it might also serve as a weapon—its owner, an old man,
holds it in his fist like a scepter. Though everything else in
the man's face, the skin, the lips, the hair, may be those
of an old man, the eyes invite comparison with those of the
young man upstairs in the attic window: while the young
man considers the things within his field of vision with
suspicion or curiosity, the old man views the world outside
his window with total indifference. Unmoved, the old man
lets his eyes follow the swaying branches, an airplane in the
sky, or the pallbearers in their braided jackets carrying a
coffin into the building through a side entrance. The sharply
bent lower branch of a plane tree takes on the shape of a
stirrup. The slanting shingled roof of the toolshed emanates

an archaic slatelike gray, and the elder bush climbing the plank wall has parallel branches that imitate the rungs of a ladder. The old man's gaze seems to postpone the coming of dusk and bathe its objects in daylight. The bays of shadow at the edges of the short, straight canal that runs through the grounds seem to frame the meanders of a great river; the trees of the long line of forest on the horizon beyond them are the masts of ships. Closer to the observer lies a strip of no-man's-land, traversed by an expressway; the inaudible cars become speedboats on a busy watercourse. The most distant point on the horizon is the bald hill behind the forest of masts; the chalk-white church becomes a lighthouse, the hilltop an atoll, and the treetops in front of it an outer reef. It's a short step into the distance, and a short step back again; long lines of fishermen's huts elsewhere on the horizon, in the harbor of another island, extend directly the lines of the old man's hand, which is resting on the windowsill of the old people's home. In the empty blue zenith above him appears the dark outline of a parachutist, revolving slowly, gliding this way and that, and finally, as a matter of course, landing on the old man's open palm in the shape of a light-winged linden seedpod, from which is hanging the "parachutist," a little ball no larger than a juniper berry.

The old man moves. He starts walking back and forth between his window and the lectern. Each time he comes to the lectern he takes the pencil and, apparently holding his breath, adds a new sign at the foot of a column; back at the window, his lookout, he exhales slowly; that seems to bring out the last colors in the grass outside, in the oblique grooves on the porter's lodge, and in a folded wheelchair.

The signs in the notebook, however, are unrelated to what is going on outside; at the most they might stand for a feathered arrow, the forked end of a branch, or the whirls of a bird plunging through the air. The old man walks back and forth without his stick—it is leaning against the wall; his gait is not a shuffling but a sauntering, a negligent thrust forward of one leg after the other, which, oddly enough in so small a space, sometimes becomes a striding. A column of words is finally added to the signs: "participate"; "occasion?"; "gather"; "separate?"

His day's work is evidently done. The old man sits down on the camp bed; wearing a loose-fitting suit and a fully buttoned shirt, he sits erect with his hands on his knees. The window is open and the roar of the Sunday-evening traffic pours in from the expressways, punctuated now and then by a backfire. Then comes a loud screech, followed at once by a crash. A brief silence is broken by screams of pain, fear, and horror, cries for help; finally a general shouting and bellowing, accompanied in the background by a mindless blowing of horns. The old man's window offers a good view of the goings-on. But he remains seated, apparently unmoved. Then by chance, in the midst of the sobbing and wailing from the scene of the accident, the institution's funeral bell starts to ring for an entirely different person. Though the clamor outside continues, now intermingled with the howling of sirens, and though the old man in his cell has raised his head to listen, he shuts his ears more and more resolutely to all that. What gradually becomes audible, drowning out the tumult, are bird calls and the flow of water in the little irrigation ditch, merging with the rustling of the trees in the park, ocean breakers, the chirping of birds, the cry of gulls. The old man on the folding bed begins to rock back and forth from the waist and to tap his thighs with his fingers in the same rhythm. He leans his head back and opens his mouth, but no sound emerges. With his dilated nostrils and protuberant eyes he resembles an old, old singer, long fallen silent, whose singing today comes only from his hearing and seeing.

The pencil lies diagonally across the book, in the small circle of light. Its upper surface is imprinted, in block letters: CUMBERLAND. The writing beneath the pencil suggests several trains waiting on parallel tracks, the words being cars and the signs locomotives. A whistle, as though to signal the trains' departure, is actually blown in the distance, prolonged by a whistle-blowing that fills the whole building.

The whistling is repeated close at hand. The window past which the lighted train rolls over a bridge is not the one in the old people's home. It, too, is open, but it is rectangular, wider than it is high, and has no sill. The walls of the room are covered with photographs of all sizes, some in frames—not mere metal strips, but carved mahogany. The pictures are all of the same person: as a shapeless infant, as a sturdy toddler, as the youthful queen of a costume ball, and finally, in a variety of poses and with different sorts of lighting, as a beauty. In almost all the pictures she is alone and—whether as infant or as young woman—always displays the same look of imperiousness and of knowing herself to be the center of attention. All the pictures betray an indomitable self-confidence, with two exceptions. In the few photos that show her resting her head on a man's shoulder, her expression is naïve or artificial; and in the one picture of a little girl with a pigtail and white stockings, sitting on a wicker chest beside a bunk bed in a nursery suggestive of a stage set—the slumped figure with her legs crossed, her hands folded in her lap, and the for-once-perplexed eyes (which appear to be looking only at a wooden penguin about the same size as herself, holding a clothes hanger in its beak and bearing the legend: CLOTHES VALET)—she seems vulnerable and forsaken.

On one wall the photographs frame a mirror showing from behind the woman as she is now, with a bend in the part of her hair. Her hair seems wet. Clad in a white dressing gown, she is sitting at a desk, bent low over a copybook the size of a ledger. Seen from the front, her real face, as opposed to the one in the photographs, seems sullen, almost hard. With lowered eyes and pursed lips, she is wielding a thick fountain pen, blind to the last yellow glow in the sky outside the window, to the basket of fruit in the dining nook, to the bunch of flowers at the head of the enormous bed in the seemingly illuminated bedroom. In spite of the block letters, her writing is almost illegible; the few characters with anything approaching a shape have the sweep of Chinese calligraphy. However, she speaks in an undertone as she writes. Her fingers covered with ink spots, an extraordinarily large lump on her middle finger, she delivers herself, more or less, of the following: "He said I was always demanding love, though I myself was totally incapable of giving love. He said that I've never been anyone's wife and never will be. He said I was restlessness personified and whoever I was with I'd never give him anything but trouble. Sooner or later I'd inspire the gentlest person in the world with a destructive urge, in the form either of homicidal frenzy or of a death wish, and convince him that this trait was his true character. He says the childlike creature who casts her spell on anyone she pleases turns out, once I've lured my victim into my child's lair, to be a monster from whose clutches there is no escape; he says I'm the witch Circe, who transformed every one of Odysseus' companions into a pig, and Odysseus himself as well. Living with me, he says, made him homesick for the fresh air of solitude and made him resolve, no, swear, never again to go near a woman. He says I brought him to the point that if the most glorious apparition made eyes at him, his only thought would be: Get lost! He asks why in all this time he has never learned to love me, why he has come to regard himself as hopelessly unlovable, and why he can't help hating himself as much as me for it. He cursed my father and mother. He cursed the place of my birth. He cursed my entire generation, calling us aimless, prematurely corrupt, profane, incapable of yearning. He said I had no interest in anything outside the two of us, no interest in work, nature, history, that I was obsessed with love, with twosomeness, and failed to understand that two people can attain happiness only with the help of something outside themselves. He says I have no ambition to achieve anything, that I lack the thirst for knowledge—which might have enabled me to understand myself through my forebears—or any longing for the unknown; he says I've been living in my apartment for ten years and still don't know the name of the mountain on the horizon, or of the river outside my window, or where the trains on the bridge out there are coming from and where they are going; he says the only place-name known to me in this city is that of the street I live on; he says the points of the compass are all the same to me, that the word 'south' means nothing to me but sea and sunshine, that if anyone mentions north or west I crinkle my nose and look bored. He says my reaction to any form of knowledge is to panic, as if someone were threatening to push me into a hostile element. He says I have no time for any person or thing other than myself, that however beautiful a thing may be, I barely take note of it and never look at it, and that as a result my conception of beauty or ugliness is unforgivably superficial; he thinks it outrageous that I find nothing worth looking at or listening to. And from this follows the worst thing of all, that with me no stability is possible—and without stability there's no everyday life. Nevertheless, he says, he has discovered that some part of me is good and great. But it shows itself only on the fringes, and I give it neither time nor space. So, he says, I should finally forget my dream of becoming part of a couple, and in that connection he quotes *Parzifal* and *King Lear* to me: 'A person of breeding does not speak of love.' And 'Love, and be silent.' ' "

Along with her monologue, the woman has concluded her from-start-to-finish indecipherable writing, in which only the often double and triple exclamation points and underlinings are clear: her reply. She rises, not abruptly, but with graceful vigor. Her pen and paper fall to the floor. She squats down, looks at them, but leaves them where they are. The room with its army of lamps and disorderly piles of television magazines distills the slightly subdued atmosphere of a Sunday evening. With wide-open eyes the woman stands in front of the large mirror. Quarreling voices are heard from an adjoining apartment. Her absent look and crouching posture give the figure in the mirror the air of an animal that has strayed into a high rise. Then suddenly she looks back over her shoulder and laughs into the void, a carefree laugh that might have been addressed to someone on the street. Lightly she slips into the other room; dressing and doing her face, she flits gracefully back and forth between the two rooms, which thanks to her parading take on the character of a grandiose suite. In no time at all she is in the doorway, ready to go out. There, to be sure, she drops her handbag and has to bend down to pick up its scattered contents. Rising to her full height, she stands for a long moment, letting herself be looked at, so to speak: no longer a displaced animal but a star. Finally, with a toss of the chin, she says to her audience: "Don't bother me with your everyday life. No one else can give you people the pleasure I give you. You all need me. And so do *you!*"

Outside a movie house displaying posters of entirely different stars stands a soldier in street uniform and tilted cap. He is flanked by a middle-aged couple outfitted for travel—umbrella in fair weather, hats. His mother has taken his arm; his father, at some distance, is covertly watching the other two from the side. The movie house is across from the railroad station; they have only stopped there for a moment, and now they are crossing the square. Here the Sunday evening is betokened by the old newspapers blowing over the asphalt or filling the trash cans to overflowing and by the fact that the handful of travelers in the station hall are far outnumbered by drunks sleeping or bellowing and groups of foreign workers in the corners. The three cross the platform to a waiting room, a separate structure situated on an island between the tracks which, though hardly bigger than a hut, has a marble doorway. The interior is rather like a parlor: curved benches and lacquered tables in which the overhead lamp is reflected. The slender stove in the corner reaches up to the ceiling. In one recess there is a miniature fountain and across from it a tiny palm tree. Instead of the usual oversize views of tourist attractions, the walls are decorated with faded landscape paintings, and the tables are equipped with ashtrays. Here, where in both rows of windows trains are perpetually stopping and starting off again, the group sits down. The parents keep their hats on and their faces remain half shaded; the soldier rolls up his cap and puts it in his trouser pocket. Bareheaded, with his scraggly short hair, his somewhat pimply forehead, and his chubby cheeks, he gives the impression of a schoolboy, but sitting there between the two others he shows no sign of being their son; while they are visibly concerned with him, his attention, his watchfulness, as it were, is directed toward the things around him, the cigar rest in the ashtray, which in his eyes takes on the shape of a mountain pass, and the bent tips of the palm leaves, groping like tentacles. Thus the soldier seems independent of the parents to the left and right of him. If he bows his head like a son, it is only as a favor to them, a pretense. His mother has the floor; his father sits silent, his expression suggests disengagement, resolute neutrality. The woman, still young in voice and bearing, speaks as follows: "I'd been hoping that army life would help you to come out of your shell. I saw you turning into the different man that you've always been deep down, the kind of man who knows the right moment for everything, the right moment to take action, the right moment to withdraw, the right moment for the right word, and who consequently becomes the one who counts, the mainspring, even when he isn't the actual leader. Instead, you're just absent, now more than ever. You mustn't suppose I care if after all these months you haven't a single stripe—I'm just disappointed that you don't make your presence felt, either in the barracks or outside. To your comrades you're a nobody; when you come into a room, nobody sees you; when you leave it, they hear the door closing and that's all; your salutes are ignored; when we asked for you, your name meant nothing to anyone; even when your father described you, and you know how well he does that, the only reaction was a shrug. At a restaurant you're still the one whose order the waitress has forgotten, and when waiting in line you're the one who gets shoved aside. You could be all alone in a room, you could be on a raised platform with a spotlight shining on you, and you'd still be overlooked. You're always absent. At home, where you've spent twenty years of your life and have hardly ever been away, nobody asks for you. Nobody remembers you, neither your teachers nor your classmates; and even your friend of those days doesn't think of me anymore as your mother but only as Frau So-and-So. Even we, your parents, when we see you find it hard to believe that it's really you. You're there and then again you're not. It's your absence that drives us away from you. Because it doesn't come natural to you, you put it on as a defense against us, against others, against the world; it's your weapon. You frighten me with your absence. Sometimes I get the feeling that you're not my child at all, that you were foisted on me. Even when you were little, I caught myself knocking at your door, as if you were a stranger. Who are you actually? Show yourself at last, let yourself be recognized. Show your other weapons, my child, the weapons that disarm, just as time and time again at the right moment you have disarmed me, or your father, or your opponent, with a glance, a question."

During his mother's speech the soldier keeps his eyes on his surroundings, as though ready to leap. If a ball were suddenly to come flying, he would catch it. During some of the woman's sentences he glanced over his shoulder at something. For a moment or two a black man on a distant bench came closer. The weak irregular jet of the fountain grew strong and seemed to be the outstanding event of the station area; the fountain became monumental. The letters on the glass door framed the view and the objects in it; a face in the window of a train, a lighted switch at the edge of the tracks, became as palpable as though seen through a telescope.

Now the waiting room is occupied by other people. The three have gone. The platforms are empty, and so are the many tracks; the rails give off a cold gleam. A last car vanishes around the long curve. After that there are only the high-rise buildings beyond the dead fields, the lighted windows almost as close together as in the old people's home. This is the time of day when most people are back from their Sunday outings, but few want to be in the dark; countless silhouettes are seen standing in the middle of rooms, motionless except for hands moving up and down with cigarettes.

The soldier has put his cap on again. Already far from the station, he is walking along the river—alone now— with giant strides, as though flying. In almost every tele- phone booth a motionless shadow. An arm that seems to have been dangling all day from a car window is pulled back. Three teenage girls are waiting in front of a house; a very small child steps out of the door. Knots of foreign workers are standing around, looking more Slavic than ever with their prominent cheekbones. In response to a homicidal look the soldier salutes, and the saluted person suddenly comes to life.

On one of the main streets—rows of lighted, yet barred shopwindows—he stands at some distance from a few others, mostly soldiers. While the others engage in conversation and a bit of shadowboxing, he takes a cookie out of his jacket pocket and eats it in a leisurely, almost ceremonious way. There is a church nearby; a poster on the wall of the bus shelter announces PILGRIMAGE TO THE HOLY LAND.

In the bus he takes a book from his other pocket and reads. Repeatedly in the course of the trip he looks up—at a pedestrian crossing or at the one good-looking girl on the bus—always for longer than needed to digest what he has been reading. The army camp, way out beyond the expressways, is invisible, recognizable only by the glaring white sentry box in a small birch forest and the barriers on either side of it. The soldier slips through in line with the others.

It's deep night. The lights go out on the airfield. A pedestrian light changes; there are no more pedestrians; the stick figures on the light are crooked. A voice comes out of a dark ground-floor window; it starts with a loud, clear word, but then becomes unintelligible, the voice of a sleeper. In the center of town, on the squares, there is hardly anything but animal sounds to be heard: the screeching of cats, the roaring of a bull in a slaughterhouse far away, the scream of a peacock in a zoo. The television sets in a shopwindow all display their test patterns. At one of the scenes of Sunday's accidents whitish sand is being strewn over blood, which in one place is still discernible, a circular, clotted, pitch-black spot, as though the victim's heart had drained just there. The light of a streetlamp shines into a café, whose chairs and tables are sharply outlined in the gloom; in one corner a basket full of leftover bread, shrunken, crusts broken, as happens to baked goods only on Sunday evenings; the few men left on the chess board have all tipped over, except the king, who stands proudly erect. A segment of the sky includes the half-moon in the shape of an apothecary's mortar, prepared to receive the pill that is the single star. A uniform rumbling fills the room, as though the city's machines had not been fully turned off and were ready to start up again at any moment.

Only in the gambling establishment have time and the outside world ceased to exist. Fluorescent tubes make it as bright as day, the thick curtains offer no gap through which to look out, and besides, it would never occur to the gamblers to raise their eyes from the cards or dice. In contrast to the depopulated world outside, the large room, the sections of which are separated by pillars, is crowded, literally black with people. Nevertheless, apart from a group of young billiards players, all beginners who have come here only to prove their courage, there is no noise. Hardly anyone speaks; there is little to be heard but the shuffling of cards, the shaking of dice, and the hum of the ventilators, one in each wall. Not a single picture; far and wide only the shimmer of green paint, rubbed dull on the baseboards by the movements of nervous heels. Even the usual plants and lone dog are missing. Cigarette butts fall thick and fast on the tile floor, the players stamp them out without looking. The only decoration in the room is the oval stucco ornament on the high ceiling, the one thing at which one of the players, invariably the loser, to be sure, occasionally takes a quick, furtive look.

There is a main table, recognizable not by its size but by the number of onlookers standing around it. It is not in the center of the room but in a corner. One of the men sitting at it is the big man; he is not among the losers. He is white-haired and smooth-skinned, as though beardless, while most of the others at the table look unshaved. Like them he is wearing a dark suit, a white shirt, and no tie. But over his suit he is wearing an almost floor-length camel's-hair coat, as though he were cold. Another thing that singles him out is that he is not sitting in a chair like the others but on a backless stool at one corner of the table. There he sits upraised, with his legs folded under him, and keeps the bank. While waiting for bets to be made—some of the apparent onlookers standing around the table turn out to be players—he shakes the dice in a rhythm suggesting an endless drumroll, summoning all present to step up and join in. The emptying of the cup is all the more sudden; a slight flick of the wrist, which sends the dice to the edge of the dice board and bouncing back again. His hands alone seem concerned with what is going on; the one always busy with the dice, the other, after the throw, with jotting down numbers, which his gold pencil seems to inscribe autonomously on a slip of paper. Otherwise, no part of him moves; the cigarette in his mouth, which he never draws on, is always relit by an assiduous henchman at his side, who also rakes in the banknotes for him—the dancing of a coin on this table is unthinkable—smooths them out, and arranges them in piles. And, like most of the gamblers here, he never orders a drink from the manager, who makes his rounds at intervals (but he invariably has a banknote from one of the piles slipped to him). He never says a word. At times he seems even more bleary-eyed and pale than the others; his hands seem to move of their own accord, as though he were asleep under his swollen eyelids. But seen from close up, his pupils are constantly darting this way and that. While shaking the dice, he is equally keeping an eye on the crackling banknotes between the fingers of one of the onlookers and on the game at the next table, where big, pallid, almost hairless fists are clutching very small cards. A blue light shines from below on the face of the solitary player farther back, plying a one-armed bandit. In mid-scream the lone girl in the noisy billiards group feels the gambler's glance, breaks off, and looks around at her companions as though for protection.

The dice are rolled again, but then they are left lying on the table. The thrower takes his watch from his vest pocket, signaling the end of the game. Others, too, open their watches. The banker tots up columns of figures, a few banknotes are distributed; he stuffs the lion's share into his coat pocket and reaches behind him for his cap, which is of the same material as his coat. But then, with his cap already on his head, he remains seated and even leans back against the wall. The others, too, remain in their places, like him almost motionless, pursuing a dream. On all sides of the table, running toward the middle, innumerable fingerprints. Even after standing up, the gambler does not leave at once, but lifts the curtain a little. He looks out into the faint early light and sees a bus loop on the edge of the city—shimmering pre-dawn wires; milk bottles singly or in pairs on the doorsteps of uniform housing-development dwellings.

The gambler seems to find no difficulty in passing from one sphere to another. After a brief look back at the black ventilator hole with its fluttering slats, he turns unhesitatingly to face the long, articulated bus whose support bars, as it drives empty into the loop, glitter like an army of spears. He takes the opposite direction from the bus, cuts across the city line, and strikes out across country. Here again, as previously on the road, he keeps looking over his shoulder, not to make sure that no one is following him, but as though expecting to see something behind him. Now and then he even spins about, as though to face an invisible group, which possibly includes the little clumps of birch trees. Making his way through rough scrubland along a rusty, abandoned railroad track, the gambler takes longer and longer strides, even jumping over a tie. Here at last he begins to speak, a mere mumble of unconnected words: "Deformed! . . . anywhere . . . on your knees . . . get caught . . . water of life . . . machine tool . . . prepare . . . no time . . . surrounded . . . adequately . . . neglected . . . bunch . . . fit subject . . . include . . . shatter . . . open up . . . track down . . . deluge . . . outright . . ." He starts to run, punching himself in the head, sticking a finger down his throat to no effect, or bending the same finger, holding it up to his temple, and going through the motions of shooting himself over and over again. Once he even turns off his path and casually rams his forehead against a tree trunk.

At the end of the track, through a strip of tall grass, whose blades seem to bar the way like swords, the gambler enters an open field of rubble, almost without vegetation, surrounded on all sides by bushes and looking like a disk inserted in the meadows on the edge of the city. The only rise is a mound made up of concrete blocks, gravel, and earth. At the side of this mound, the gambler sits down on a stone, looks at the packet of banknotes beside him, and continues his mumbling: "Money, you've always been my mainstay. No money, no world. Money, you have not only been my parachute, which up until now has never failed to open, but also my airship, ready to take off in any direction, reliable and crashproof. Money, my last resort and only clear idea. Money, my only ray of hope!" Suddenly he stops and in the same tone of voice addresses a little clump of pale-yellow grass, swaying at eye level: "I must get away from here, no matter where to. To a place where I can grieve and have something to grieve for. To a place where loyalty will again count for something. I need danger. There may be danger here, too, but I don't feel it. What was that dream I had? I was sitting at the table, I had sat there every evening for ten years, waiting for the others. And when they came, they sat down at other tables, not out of hostility but because nobody knew me. What has become of me? They call me the 'artist,' but I'm only the archenemy, the gambler. Instead of embodying the world, I am the point where lovelessness is concentrated. I am the point at the tip of the lance, a bundle of whiplashes. Instead of being many-sided and disarming, I am cutting, sterile, and aggressive. I am so dependent on constant presence of mind that I'm not present at all, neither for anyone else nor for myself. 'You're not there!' All the women I've ever loved have said that. Loved? I never loved anyone. They call me the freest of men, but I'm just indifferent, volatile. I say what I like and go where I please, but it gives me no feeling of freedom; I feel only the injustice and privation I've suffered. None of them knows how often I say to myself: Shut up and stay put. They call me a king, but I'm just a liar and a hypocrite. My generosity is really condescension, my indulgence and attitude of live and let live is disloyalty, my aloofness contempt. Instead of being the king of life, as they say, I'm an enemy of mankind—a scoundrel when I'm gambling; and when I'm not gambling, a soulless sneak."

The gambler looks around, taking in the strip of wand-like alders, the stunted silver birches, and the lone spruce sighing in the wind at the edge of the disk; takes two stones from the pile, knocks them together; and, swaying his torso back and forth, carries on with his mumbled singsong: "Make a fresh start. I say that today for the first time, and I've never heard anyone say it in earnest. Begin a new life. But if I only say it to myself, I don't mean it. Nobody hears the things I say to myself, so they don't count. Love. I'll take time and let myself be diverted by love. Give me the saving grief that will finally tell me which way to go. Inflict it on me. No longer will the steel pen get stuck between my ribs. Renew the wound each day, dearest, my one and only, whether man or woman. Reject me if need be, but tell me why; scorn me, mock me, make me open up and cease to be alone. Embitter me, make a kernel grow within me, make me fruitful. Spell it out. Give it to me in writing. That's it. To make me mean what I say, to assure myself that what I say will be heard and will therefore stand fast, I will spell it out and give it to myself in writing. Even if what is sung does not exist, the voice of the singer does."

Making what he has said true, he writes in his pad with his gold pencil; this he does with such emphasis that his shoulders begin to spin and his whole body to shake. He gets up from his stone and washes his face and hands in one of the many puddles that abound in the scrubland, as though the ground below them were frozen all year long. Near the puddle there is a single clump of grass with broad, flat blades that splay out in all directions like shocks of hair. It is lit up from the side by the first rays of the sun and stirred by the early breeze. The blades are transparent and clearly show their fine ribs running all the way to the tips, and the shadow of one blade falls on the next blade's trail of light. The longer we look at the clump as it trembles, shakes, and sways, the more sounds converge in it, each connected to the next—the screech of the crow overhead, the train whistle on the horizon, the beating of carpets in the housing development, the rat-tat-tat of the rifle range —and in the end we get the impression that the sounds of a cosmos are being made in the center of the clump, in its roots. The intensified movement that runs through the blades of grass does not result from the wind alone.

In similar light, the old man is standing on a ladder in the garden of the old people's home. He looks over his shoulder as if he senses that someone is looking at him and he wants to answer the look. His ladder is much too big for the little tree it is leaning against, and the tree bends to one side. With his pruning shears he cuts out the crown. His way of looking around, his quick decision, and his movements show that he is an expert. The branches fall all over him, on the brim of his hat and on his shoulders.

After vanishing into the shed beside the rainbow-colored beehouse, he reappears without his blue apron. His tie and the cape over his shoulders suggest that he is going on a trip. He bends down to the rivulet that runs through the garden and washes his hands in it. Without a stick he makes his way to the gate; the members of the staff greet him when they see him coming. The director, whose car door has just been opened by a subordinate, takes his hat off to the old man and wishes him a pleasant and profitable day in town, speaking as one might to a person of importance, but also, with mock respect, to an old crackpot. It seems likely that they will all exchange smiles behind his back.

Out on the square he turns back to look at the chapel that occupies the central part of the block-long building. One of its double doors is ajar; in the cleft there is nothing but black. While he jots down something in his breviary-like notebook, an elderly couple hobbles past behind him. In the same loud, hard-of-hearing voice, they both say at once: "He's writing again."

On a busy street in the center of town the old man stops and squats down over a cracked paving stone. He blows the dust off it and spreads one of the thin, still-empty pages of his notebook over it and starts rubbing with a lead pencil. Little by little the outlines of a letter, then of two more letters, appear on the paper: AVT, a fragment of a Roman inscription, meaning uncertain—"or?"; "but?"; "autumn?" He is oblivious of the onlookers, more and more of whom gather around him, as if he were a famous sidewalk painter; not even the hissing and sparkling of a hot-air balloon hovering over the street distracts their attention.

Alone again, the old man is standing on a carless square, at the foot of a statue. It is a woman with her head thrown back as though in a scream; the line of the throat catches the eye; seen from below, sparkling with particles of mica, her breast against the sky becomes a mountain pass which draws the eye into the distance and in which light becomes substance. Sheltered by his cape, the decipherer draws a quick stroke in his notebook and beside it sets the word "exit." As he does so, red blotches sprout on his cheeks and his face takes on a look of excitement surprising in a man his age, an excitement that reminds one of a messenger boy sent on an errand for the first time. In the next moment he will stammer out his news, an event which he himself has brought about. But then, looking straight ahead, he lets himself be diverted. Escorted by two normal persons, a group of idiot children is crossing the square, making incomprehensible gurgling, trilling, cheering sounds; their way of walking, with knees strangely bent, gives their procession, at first sight, the appearance of a sack race. Some of them are wearing head guards like hockey players. The old man looks straight at them; amazement, delight, or idiocy is reflected in his face. He and the group belong together; all of a sudden he has come across something of whose existence he was not even aware. Openmouthed, he contemplates his tribe and puts his notebook away. While looking at them, he recruits additional members, for somewhere on the square a second onlooker follows his eyes, and, puzzled at first, then understanding, a third . . . The old man trails after his tribe. His hobbling gait is like that of the children, but not so laborious.

It is a different procession that impels the soldier to start off. He is far out in a suburb, as though in the vicinity of a borderline, guarding an imperiled war memorial. In front of him an expressway, beyond it a wide river, easy to cross at this point, made up of several swift watercourses separated by strips of rubble. Wearing mottled combat fatigues and a steel helmet, he is carrying a rifle with mounted bayonet; at his feet a crackling radiotelephone. His eyes are hidden by the shadow of his helmet.

For a long time there are no passersby, only the roaring of the cars, many trucks among them. Then some children pass on their way home from school. One of the boys stations himself under the soldier's nose, the tips of his shoes touching the tips of the soldier's boots, and stays there until the soldier's fingers suddenly start drumming on his belt buckle; a moment later, the sentry is alone again. Next, at an intersection within his field of vision, a small group of pedestrians appears, whose festive dress radiates an eerie splendor in this workaday landscape. This because of the dark colors—the black of the men's suits and the uniform violet of the women's attire, even of their hats and handbags. This group is only the advance guard; more and more of the holidaymakers follow, in pairs, in clusters, and finally in a swarm that overflows the footpath and takes up part of the road. It is in no sense a parade that passes the war memorial; these people don't even seem to notice it or the soldier. Far from marching, they seem to be strolling, taking the air, as it were. Their self-absorption, their easy chatter, their unconstrained gestures, the glow of contentment in the eyes even of the children show that their festival, though drawing to a close, is not yet over. It is not a wedding or a baptism but a public religious festival, the just-experienced ritual of which continues to hold them together as they talk about purely secular concerns far from their place of worship. It is a great festival observed only by this particular group, an offshoot of a foreign race. Of this there are no outward indications, but only their sense of time, which is radically different from that of the figures in the cars speeding by. It is most apparent in the young women, who are all wearing high-heeled boots and costumes with short, tight skirts, which shimmer as they pass; for them this is in part a festival of the flesh. As soon as they get home, each one of them, the giantess as well as the midget, will give herself to her companion, and in their rooms the language of union will prevail until nightfall. Moving slowly along the road, glassy-eyed in the light, they are making ready for the man who will become their husband in the darkened tent.

The soldier is no longer standing by the memorial. Only his rifle is leaning against the pedestal. The radio-telephone is silent. His steel helmet is lying on the river-bank, half buried in sand, full of egg-shaped pebbles and pinecones. The murmur of the water, the thundering of a train, and the clattering of a helicopter are caught in it.

With rippling hair, the soldier runs through an underpass, which is so long that for a time the end of it is hidden from sight. He passes young soldiers like himself coming from the opposite direction, all carrying identical plastic bags, on their way back to the barracks from the supermarket; though few are engaged in conversation, none notices him. Two girls, walking arm in arm as though for protection, also look through him, as if they had eyes only for the exit. He stops once, takes the dagger from his felt boot, and scrapes away a tiny inscription, almost obscured by the grooves in the concrete, from the wall of the tunnel; after that, no longer in a hurry, he takes his book from his hip pocket and, now striding straight ahead, immerses himself in it.

Emerging from the underpass, the soldier is in a different part of the world. The hedges by the roadside have evergreen, cup-shaped leaves, gleaming far and wide in the light of a southern sun, and the cone of rubble on the horizon is traversed by a dried-out, petrified riverbed. As he walks, the soldier puts on dark glasses and undoes the zipper of his jacket; behind him, far far away, hardly distinguishable from the clouds, there is a northern, snow-covered mountain.

Her back to the window, whose drawn curtain captures the sun, the young woman is sitting on a suitcase in the attitude she had taken as a child when sitting on the linen chest in her bedroom. Just as silent, hands folded in her lap, her legs crossed, she stares into space, blind to her surroundings. Instead of being worn in a pigtail, her hair hangs loose, and instead of a dress with enormous buttons, she is wearing a tailored suit. Silent, yes, but with frequent interruptions. As though at predetermined intervals, she honors the outside world with an outburst which may be serious and may be playacting: "You people! Always telling

me to change. But I don't *want* to change . . . But I don't
want to work. Work would only destroy me. Work makes
people stupid. And you, too . . . But I don't *want* to know
anything. I don't want to go to museums, and I don't want
to learn a foreign language. I like to see pictures by chance,
without planning to, no matter where, and I can only be
myself and act like myself in my own language. I can't love
in a foreign language. Knowledge would destroy me the
same as work, it would make me cold and stupid. When I
was a child, the moment you people started lecturing me
I stopped my ears. One reason why I was never able to read
your books of knowledge was the way the sentences are
constructed; all I could get out of them was the droning of
the lecturer. You lecturers are sucking my blood. Your
knowledge shouldn't be allowed. Your knowledge is taboo.
Admittance to knowledge should be prohibited. You clever
people should keep quiet about your knowledge and come
out with it only in cases of urgency, and then in the form
of poems or songs . . . But I don't *want* to go out. What
should I do out of doors? I need my ambience and it's here
that I can have it. Walk, run, ride, travel. With the words
'walk' and 'out of doors,' you've always driven me into the
farthermost corner of the room, behind the folding screen.
Every time I went on a trip with my parents I fell asleep
the moment I sat down in the car, and I don't remember
one thing about any trip except an Eskimo pie somewhere
or a seatless toilet in some gas station. Trains stink even if
they're called Loreley; and even if airplanes are called Trans
World and fly across the international dateline, all they can
do is take me to a concrete runway, where the skyline of
the identical city will only make me homesick. I have no

desire whatever to see your Tristan da Cunha or your Ant-
arctic or your river What's-its-name, where Plato is supposed
to have taken a walk. I don't believe in foreign wonders.
All your sacred springs and grottoes and trees should be
turned into playgrounds with paper boats and flashlights
shining into every oracle cleft. And don't bother me with
the grandeur of nature. Even the words—'linden,' 'rose,'
'fleecy clouds'—stick in my craw, for one thing because
they were done to death in the rubbish we used to write in
our poetry albums . . . Only for love would I leave here;
only for love would I travel day and night, climb mountains,
ride horseback, swim, always in a straight line, straight
ahead, without any of your detours . . ."

The last part of her declaration is addressed to a fly on
the back of her hand. She jumps up and lets the fly out the
window. In so doing, she catches sight of a taxi in front of
the building. It seems to have been waiting there for some
time; the driver, standing beside it smoking, reaches through
the open window and blows the horn emphatically. The
woman runs into the living room, where she consults the
video horoscope for the day: "This is your day of decision.
Don't miss the favorable moment. Make up your own mind.
Accept help only in the event of a crisis. A crisis is more
than a bind that you can get out of unaided. You will know
it's a crisis when you try as usual to get help from the first
person who happens to be around and find that you can't."
She goes to the mirror and runs her hand over her cheek;
her eyes are dilated, her shoulders are crooked. She clings
to the frame of the mirror with both hands, as though fearing
to be dragged out of her four walls to the ends of the earth.

But already she is on her way to the taxi, transformed

after a few steps, as though stepping onto the stage from the wings. She moves vigorously, swinging her aluminum suitcase as though it were empty. Her eyes widened by the wind, her nostrils flaring, her teeth flashing. Mollified at seeing her there, the driver hastens to relieve her of her suitcase, which in his hands seems twice as heavy as before. As she gets in, she turns around toward the building—a showy concrete façade with dark-stained wooden balconies and roof gardens planted with stands of dwarf cypresses—and exhales audibly. At the same time, she unclenches her fist and a bunch of keys falls to the ground. Opening fanwise, they lie on the sidewalk near a lone ginkgo leaf, blown from far away, a small leaf with a very long stem, more like a flower petal than the leaf of a large tree.

The taxi speeds away. Already it has disappeared around the corner. Then, on the highways, come scenes of indecision: change of lanes to the left; back to the middle; change of direction, sudden hairpin turn; reverse gear on the open road.

At length the taxi stops at a crossroads; the light turns green, but the cab stays right there, while cars pass on both sides. High overhead, hanging from wires: a traffic light, constantly swaying, despite its great size, in an unearthly rhythm which enables it at certain moments to embody a menacing thousand-eyed goddess glaring red-yellow-and-green in all directions and demanding human sacrifices.

The gambler is lying face down in the meadow grass under a springtime sun. The place where he is lying is scrubland even more remote than where he was before, without puddles or mounds of rubble; the few trees on the fringes are all stunted, most of them withered; the only sound to be heard is the whistling of the wind, which, unobstructed by any settlement or plantation, blows evenly from desert spaces; the man would seem to have been wounded and to have dragged himself to this place where he thought no one would find him. And yet there was once a civilization here; behind the trees there is a ruin that might be mistaken for a hill or a great rock; a white-rimmed hole that was once a portal and the lower half of what was once a window. But it is not a place of pure antiquity; to one side of the recumbent gambler there is a stone fireplace— the ashes are still fresh, showing the traces of a few drops that did not develop into a proper rainfall—and on the other a rubber band, as usual shaped like a figure eight.

Suddenly the gambler jumps up and goes to a box tree, at the foot of which a stone surrounded by clumps of grass indicates the former boundary of the estate. Setting his foot on the stone, he contemplates the box tree, which is un- usually large for its kind, at once delicate and untamed, and towers far above him. The tips of the branches, which have not been pruned for a long time, have splayed out into untidy tufts, all pointing in different directions like the clusters of road signs at the ends of the earth. The one wild shoot in the crown, as long as an arrow and crooked, moves' incessantly, nodding in the direction of a bare tree which, cloaked with ivy from top to toe and bereft of branches, is no longer recognizable as any particular kind of tree and looks rather like an unkempt post. It fans out at the top and the ivy mingles with tree shoots; the post seems to have a nest on top of it. No, there really is a nest. Something is moving in it, something climbs over the edge, a peregrine falcon—possibly fledged only a few days ago in the north —recognizable by its almost eagle-sized, storm-cloud-gray outline, out of which peer round yellow eyes. It shows no sign of wanting to fly away but just sits there with smooth, unruffled plumage, even its eyes unmoving, not at all ready to start out, settling down to a long rest after a long journey. But something happens inside the beholder on the ground: what seems at first to be a tic or grimace turns out to be a laugh, a quiet laugh that spreads over his whole face. He hasn't laughed like that since he was a baby. He breaks into a slow run, which doesn't even make the falcon in its nest turn its head.

Running, the gambler turns around from time to time and looks at his surroundings. Barely a moment seems to have passed and already he sees the first sign of human life, a slip of paper that scouts have stuck on a bramblebush. On it is written in a childlike hand: "Follow this sign." He turns in a different direction and a moment later sees another slip with the same words, this one in the vicinity of some houses, woven into the wire mesh of a trash container. He heads back into the thicket and in the next moment comes across a group of men and women in track suits, doing knee bends at the knee-bend station of a fitness course. Again the gambler runs off and a moment later, in a parklike cemetery on the edge of the city, a funeral procession crosses his path. Bells start ringing, the procession circles around a mausoleum, and he joins it, welcomed with a nod by a stranger. At the graveside he takes his leave of the stranger and runs out of the cemetery. In the bustling inner city, he keeps up a steady pace. Just once, on a short open stretch, he stops for no reason, so abruptly that several dice fall to the sidewalk. He stops their roll, gathers them up, and disappears around the corner. He seems to have doubled back. And, indeed, the vapor trails in the sky are moving in a different direction, a cigarette butt is rolling in another, a young music student is walking in another with her instrument case, and a toy motorcar, controlled by an invisible hand, is careering across the asphalt in still another. The runner looks back over his shoulder and cries out: "Follow me!"

The train in the middle of the city, two steps from the department store, also seems like a toy. There isn't any station, the tracks it is standing on merge with a marketplace right after the last car, and this enhances the toylike impression. But the train is crowded, and more and more people—unlike streetcar passengers, loaded with baggage —come running and get in. Like certain international expresses, it is made up of sections of different trains. The locomotive is far ahead of the platform. The unusual length of the train, and still more the excitement and bewilderment of the passengers, who cannot be seasoned travelers, give it for a moment the air of a special train, reserved for a group of emigrants or pilgrims from all over the country.

It is still high noon; the noonday, springtime light shines most brilliantly on the rounded tops of the cars. A signal rings out—not a train whistle, more like the tooting of an ocean liner, so long-drawn-out that a child on the platform treats himself to a kind of radio play by rhythmically stopping and unstopping his ears. But, surprisingly at the departure of so long a train, few people have come to say goodbye, and hardly anyone is looking out the open windows. Consequently, the gambler has no need to twine his way through a crowd as he runs past the market stalls; he is able to head straight for the compartment, which is reached not through a corridor but directly from outside. The door is thrown open for him even before he gets there, and closes after him like that of a funicular cabin once it is loaded to capacity.

Yet a number of seats are still vacant after he has sat down. There are only three other persons, who, though thrown together at random, seem to acquiesce in the arrangement. With the gambler the group is complete. The woman at the window does not favor him with so much as a glance—her attention is concentrated on her aluminum suitcase, as though it were in danger; pencil in hand, the old man across from her is immersed in his notebook; and the soldier's back is turned, for he is standing at the door as though to guard it. True enough, some others try to get in: first a loudmouthed couple, who at the sight of the four fall silent and go away; then a priest in travel dress who, after a greeting all around with one foot already on the threshold, vanishes as though to resume his greetings in the next compartment. Only a child strong enough to open the door by himself pushes past the soldier, and his parents have to stick their heads in and order him out with the words: "Not there. Somewhere else." The child complies with a shrug.

The hubbub outside dies away. But the train doesn't move. There's plenty of time. The soldier sits down, pulls himself up again as though in expectation—not of an event but of a first word. It's the woman who turns quite casually to the others and says: "When my childhood was over I began to wander around. I left the house and went farther and farther away, until I didn't know where I was anymore. When they caught me in some small town or out in the country, I didn't know my name and address. I usually took the train, never one that was going very far, always a local; no matter where it was going, I never bought a return ticket. What did I do when I arrived there? They told me I just sat around in the waiting room at the last stop or on the loading platform, and sometimes at the edge of a field, in a gravel pit, or by the side of a brook, regardless of the season. People began to notice me because of the way I'd sit there for hours—before that, when I was wandering around, it seems I walked like someone who knew his way and was going somewhere. Men often stopped their cars and told me to get in, but none of them touched me, they never laid a finger on me; there was never any conversation, because my answer to everything was the same: I don't know. So they took me to the police. I couldn't be a tramp, that was out of the question; even the village constables came out from behind their partitions when they saw me, and all of a sudden they stopped talking dialect. I always had plenty of money on me. And that is what made them think I was crazy. Instead of sending me home, they took me to an institution. There I was exhibited to students in a lecture hall shaped like an amphitheater. The professor showed me off, not because I was sick but because it was me. Though I only answered his rehearsed questions with yes or no, he always shook my hand with both of his and held the door open for me when my act was done. The students were crazy about me, too. My wanderings can't have made me very happy, because often when they found me sitting there I'd be crying or even shouting for help—but my act must have opened the eyes of the onlookers to something they'd never known before. While the mental patients were performing, I'd be sitting in the cubicle waiting my turn, and I'd hear the listeners coughing or laughing, but when I appeared, they'd all fall silent. They didn't feel sorry for me, they envied me. What they heard about me filled them with longing. If only, instead of moving in crowds through familiar streets, they could wander around like me in a dream and alone. My adventures made them long, not for other continents, but for the towns and villages nearby, which up until then had meant nothing to them. Thanks to me, the names took on a resonance and the places became possible destinations. Though I was standing there bare-legged in an institutional gown, for them I was a heroine. And it's true that, though actually I wasn't so very well off, I was better off than those people, who thought they were well off. One of you was there, too, as a visiting student. He only attended my demonstration because he thought I was the kind of person that moved him. He came because he respected me."

Something of hers falls on the floor. The soldier bends down. It is a fountain pen with a mother-of-pearl cap. As he turns it slowly in his hand, the light from outside seems to shine through the cap. A jolt runs through the train, and it pulls out under two trees, the one close to the track, the other by the side of the parallel road. Their branches have become intertwined so as to form an arch, though an irregular one, because the tree beside the track has been pruned to make room for the wires and the pylon, with the result that the arch has scorched or bare spots that make it look like the tusk of a mammoth. The clouds in the breach are diesel smoke mixed with soot, and the birds swerve to avoid them. The deserted platform glitters for a moment; on a high-rise tower the sign appears: HOTEL EUROPA.

At first the four in the compartment stop whatever they are doing. The gambler has a cigarette between his lips and his lighter in his hand. The soldier has a finger in his closed book. The old man, his pencil point at the ready but motionless, holds his notebook in such a way as to show the letters CUMBERLAND on the pencil. Pocket mirror in hand, the young woman stops freshening her lipstick. Further speech seems unauthorized for the present. The silence adds to their contentment. Only the woman looks questioningly from one to the other; she is the only one of the four whose face is not turned toward the window. Outside, there has been a quick succession of short tunnels and viaducts. Then, though there has been no noticeable change in the vegetation or the shapes of the houses, the light seems different, perhaps because the view of the sky is less obstructed. The train, which for a time was running at high speed like a transcontinental express, has begun to stop as frequently as a streetcar. The track is no longer running parallel to the road; for a time it skirted fields and woods, but lately it has been running straight through a forest. Hardly anyone has been getting on, but crowds of passengers have been getting out at every stop and invariably forming processions that march off on identical roads, heading for village churches miles away, on identical hilltops. At one station—actually no more than a shelter in the woods—just one person gets off, and vanishes into the woods with his worker's briefcase. Convinced that this was their last fellow passenger, the woman—who has also turned toward the window by now—reaches for the door handle. The old man restrains her with a quick shake of his head. A far from empty train, coming in the opposite direction, stops on the other track, and a group of screaming schoolchildren comes trooping down the center aisle. As the train starts up again, the old man raises his surprisingly high voice in a chant, every word of which can be heard above the hubbub: "In the childhood of peoples, unknown countries came into existence beyond the mountains and the oceans. They had names, but nobody knew where they were. Only their direction was more or less certain. The sources of the Nile were south, the Caucasus east, the legendary Atlantis west, and Ultima Thule north. Then came trading ships and wars of conquest, then came history, and then—violently, by leaps and bounds—came the adulthood of the peoples and it exploded the legends of childhood geography. The sources of the Nile were muddied, the peaks of the Caucasus reduced from heavenly heights to their actual dimensions, and Ultima Thule dislodged from its place as the kingdom at the end of the world. No Atlantis will ever again rise out of the sea. But the names remained; in epics and songs they took on a fantastic power that gave life to the realm of legend. Since then Paradise as the source of the Tigris and Euphrates and the landing of Noah's ark on Mount Ararat after the flood have been all the more real, and the infant Moses in his basket will float for all time in the slowly flowing Nile. The name is the guest of reality. In much the same way, we in our childhood gave our few favorite places faraway names; that was how the brook at the edge of the cow pasture, where we roasted potatoes under a tree in the rain, came to be called Lethe or River of Forgetfulness, how a few spindly vines came to be transposed into the Amazonian jungle, how the cliff behind the house came to be a foothill of the Sierra Nevada, how the wild lilies on top of it took on Indian colors and the hole in the garden hedge became the entrance to our New World. We, too, are grown up now, and all the names from those days, without exception, are null and void. We, too, have a history, and what was then, in those days, cannot be retrieved by any changing of names. I don't believe that those days could be brought back, even if that brook had broadened into a river, even if those vines had turned into unbreakable lianas, even if a real Apache were standing on top of the cliff where the lilies used to be. But I still believe, in earnest and no longer in play, in the power of places. I believe in places, not the big ones but the small, unknown ones, in other countries as well as our own. I believe in those places without fame or name, best characterized perhaps by the fact that *nothing* is there, while all around there is *something*. I believe in the power of those places because nothing happens there *anymore* and nothing has happened there *yet*. I believe in the oases of emptiness, not removed from fullness, but in the midst of it. I am certain that those places, even if not physically trodden, become fruitful time and again through our decision to set out and our feeling for the journey. I shall not be rejuvenated there. We shall not drink the water of life there. We shall not be healed there. We shall simply have been there. Over a stretch of rotten plank road, past a wilderness of rusty carpet frames, we shall have gone there. The grass there will have trembled as only grass can tremble, the wind will have blown as only the wind can blow, a procession of ants through the sand will have been a procession of ants, the raindrops in the dust will have taken on the incomparable form of raindrops in the dust. In that place, on the foundations of emptiness, we shall simply have seen the metamorphosis of things into what they are. Even on the way, merely because we are looking at it, a rigid blade of grass will have begun to sway, and conversely, in the presence of a tree, our innermost being will for the moment have taken on the form of that tree. I need those places and—hear now a word seldom used by an old man—I *long* for them. And what does my longing want? Only to be appeased."

In the course of his speech the weather has changed several times, alternating between sunshine and rain, high wind and calm, as in April. One river crossed by the train, hardly a trickle between gravel banks, is followed by another, a roaring, muddy flood, which is perhaps only the next meander of the first. As so often on branch lines, the stations are farther and farther apart. Once, the train has stopped in open country. The wind was so strong that from time to time the heavy car trembled. Withered leaves, pieces of bark, and branches crashed against the window. When at last the train started up again, the lines of raindrops in motion crossed those of waiting time.

Surprisingly for a place so far out in the country, there are many tracks at the station they arrive at. All end at a concrete barrier; with the exception of the rails on either side of the platform, which have been polished smooth, all are brown with rust. The station is in an artificial hollow; a steep stairway leads out of it. The soldier carrying the woman's suitcase, the four climb it together, more slowly than the few other people, all of whom are at home here. But even the newcomers are sure of the way. On leaving the ticket hall through a swinging door, they turn without hesitation in the direction indicated by the gambler, who has taken the lead. After crossing an area of bare ground and sparse, stubbly grass, suggesting an abandoned cattle pen or circus ground, they find themselves at the edge of a large forest. The trees in its dark depths seem at first sight to be covered with snow; in reality they are white birches. Here the four hesitate before crossing a kind of border, the dividing line between the yellowish clay of the open field and the black, undulating, springy peat soil. The peat bog and the forest rooted in it are also several feet higher than the field. Instead of a path cut through the earth wall there are several small wooden ladders, to one of which the gambler directs his followers with an easy gesture, showing that this is a man who gets his bearings without difficulty wherever he goes. He climbs up last, and once on top resumes leadership. Strolling through the woods—there is no underbrush between the birches—all four turn around in the direction of the station, toward which passengers are converging from all sides, all goose-stepping in a single file, though there is plenty of room in the field. Seen through the white trees, the shacklike structure seems to be somewhere in the taiga.

The forest is bright with birch light. The trees stand in beds of moss, as a rule several in a circle, as though growing from a common root. As one passes, they revolve in a circle dance that soon makes one dizzy. Over a footpath that suddenly makes its appearance—white stones sprinkled over the black ground—the four emerge at length into a wide clearing, announced some time earlier by the substitution of berry bushes for moss and by the widening middle strip of grass in the path. By now the path has become so wide that the four are able to walk abreast. On the threshold of the clearing, each of the four, on his own impulse, pauses for a moment; the woman has taken the arm of the old man, who nods his assent. Now they are fanning out in different directions, as though no longer needing a leader.

The clearing is rather hilly, shaped like a moraine spit thrust into the peat bog, and so large that the herd of deer at the other end goes right on grazing though the arrival of the newcomers has been far from soundless. Only the stag has raised his light-brown head like a chieftain. For a moment, his widely scattered herd looks like a tribe of Indians. In the middle of the clearing there is a small lake, which at first seems artificial but then—with its islands of rushes and black muddy banks, marked with all manner of animal tracks—proves to be a bog pool. Only at one point, at the tip of the moraine, so to speak, can the pool be reached dry-shod over gravel outcrops, and here its water, instead of presenting an opaque, reflecting surface, is perfectly transparent. The bright pebbles at the bottom stand out all the more clearly thanks to the glassy streaks in the water of the spring which emerges underground from the moraine and can be followed as it twines its way through the gravel to the lake which it feeds. This is also the place for a hut built of weathered, light-gray boards, shot through with amber-yellow or reddish-brown trails of resin, and for a strangely curved uphill-and-downhill boat dock that juts out over the water like a roller coaster.

Here, one by one, they all gather. The woman, the old man, and the soldier look on as the gambler fishes an enormous bunch of keys out of his coat pocket, unlocks the padlock on the hut, throws the door wide open, unlocks the glass-and-metal compartment inside it, and, after turning a last key, drives out in a car that gets longer and longer: a camper. Birch branches—camouflage and ornament in one—slide off the top.

He pushes open the back door, sets up a folding table on the grass, and spreads a white tablecloth over it. The soldier hastens to help him and brings four chairs from inside the vehicle. But for the time being no one sits down. The old man vanishes purposefully through the trees, the gambler goes into his camper, and the woman, again with her silver suitcase, signals the soldier to follow her to the boat dock. Standing behind him with scissors and comb that she has taken out of her suitcase, she changes his hairstyle. Then with a quick gesture she bids him take off his uniform and, repeatedly stepping back to scrutinize not so much the soldier as her handiwork, dresses him in civilian clothes, likewise out of her suitcase. She keeps tugging and pulling and plucking at the soldier, who doesn't seem to mind; his transformation from a chubby-cheeked bumpkin to a smooth, ageless cosmopolitan, dressed for summer and ready for anything, seems perfectly natural; only his eyes, when he turns back toward the woman, are as grave as ever; behind the happily smiling woman, ever so pleased with herself, they see the old man, who has just stepped bareheaded out of the woods, his hat full of mushrooms. While the woman takes an awl—she has everything she needs in the suitcase—and makes an extra hole in the soldier's belt, the old man, sitting beside them on the bank, cleans his varicolored mushrooms.

By then the table has been set for all. The gambler in

the camper also seems changed, not only because he is officiating at the stove in his shirtsleeves and wearing a flowered apron, but also because for cooking he has put on a pair of half-moon glasses. It is only when he suddenly looks over the edges that his glance seems as cold and dangerous as it used to. In the cramped galley he moves with the grace of a born cook—carefully wiping the glasses, putting the plates in the oven to warm, reaching for the bunches of herbs hanging from the ceiling—and shuffles in and out of the camper as though he had been running a restaurant for years.

Meanwhile, the woman and the soldier are at the table waiting. The old man is sitting on a mossy bank with his canvas-covered notebook, inscribing his columns as though in accompaniment or response to the kitchen sounds. Then he too sits motionless, though without expectation, his strikingly upright posture attributable solely to the place or the light; there is no wind, but his cape is puffed out. A bottle of wine is cooling in the spring at his feet.

Now all four are at the table and the meal is over. The glasses are still there, but only the old man is drinking wine; the gambler and the woman are smoking; the soldier has moved a short distance away; resting one heel on the knee of the other leg, he is twanging a Jew's harp rendered invisible by the hand he is holding over it—isolated chords with such long pauses between them that in the end we stop expecting a tune. As though in response to the music, the old man puts his wineglass down after every swallow, or waits with the glass in midair. Under his gaze the open back door of the camper turns into a cave, while the shingle roof of the boathouse becomes vaulted and shimmers like the scales of the fish that dart to the surface of the pool after scraps of food. Now the entire clearing has the aspect of a garden where time no longer matters. The only sounds to be heard are garden sounds, the fluttering of the tablecloth, the splashing of a fish, the brief whirring and chirping of a bird among the ferns at the edge of the forest. The clouds drift across a sky which becomes so high that space seems to form a palpable arch overhead. The blue between the clouds twists and turns and is reflected down below in the water, in the grass, and even in the dark bog soil.

The woman and the old man, who have taken their clothes off behind the camper, run down to the lake without a trace of embarrassment; the old man starts his run with a jump—like a child—and his way of running is equally childlike; the woman waits a moment, as though to give him a head start, and overtakes him at the brink of the water. The gambler and the soldier, each with a toothpick in his mouth, watch as the two swim out into the pond. The water is warm. The woman turns to the aged swimmer beside her and, speaking as though they were strolling down a path together, says: "I wish I could just stay here. Any other place I can think of would be too hot or too cold, too light or too dark, too quiet or too noisy, too crowded or too empty. I'm afraid of any new place and I hate all the old ones. In the places I know, dirt and ugliness are waiting for me; in the unknown ones, loneliness and bewilderment. I need this place. Yes, I know: it's only on the move that I feel completely at home. But then I need a place where I can spread out. Tell me of one woman who lives entirely out of suitcases and I'll tell you about all the little things you can't help noticing the moment she arrives—a framed photograph here, a toothbrush there. I need my place, and that takes time. I wish I could stay here forever."

Her swimming companion dives under; when he comes up, he has the face of a wrinkled infant. He answers in a voice made deep by the water, which resounds over the surface of the lake: "That wish cannot be fulfilled. And if it could be, it would bring no fulfillment in the long run. Whenever in my life I have thought I arrived, at the summit, in the center, *there*, it has been clear to me that I couldn't stay. I can only pause for a little while; then I have to keep going until the day when it may be possible to be *there* somewhere else for a little while. Existence for me has never been more than a little while. There is no permanence in fulfillment, here or anywhere else. Places of fulfillment have hurt me more than any others; I have come to dread them. It's no good getting used to staying in one place; wherever it is, fulfillment can't last. It loses its magic before you know it, and so does the place. *It* is not here. We are not *there*. So let's get going. Away from here. Onward. It's time."

The garden has undergone a transformation while the swimmer was speaking. Though the light is unchanged, the lake has taken on a late-afternoon look. The spring has almost dried up and the water level has fallen, uncovering the usual junk—tires, metal rods, whole bicycles—along with bleached, barkless tree trunks. The skeleton of some animal appears in the underbrush at the edge of the forest, and elsewhere a collapsed shooting bench comes to light; prematurely fallen leaves are blown over the springtime lake, and those soot-gray spots in the hollows are deposits of old snow. The clouds grow longer and are joined together by vapor trails of the same color; the faded scrap of newspaper in the bushes shows a distinct date; and that importunate noise is the persistent blowing of horns on an expressway.

The clearing is deserted, the boathouse sealed. The swimmers have left no trace in the wind-ruffled lake. Only the mud bank reveals the prints of bare feet and of the camper's tires, vanishing in the gravel path as it mounts the moraine.

The four have been on the road a long time. As they sit in their camper with legs outstretched, it's plain that they feel at home on the move. The gambler is at the wheel, the woman beside him is watching him; the old man and the soldier sit facing each other on the back benches, as in a minibus or cab. It's not only the raised seats that give them the impression that they have been climbing; the light as well is an upland light, clear and spacious. And instead of a landscape, the naked sky appears in the side windows, yellow with sunset, hazy as though from smoke but in reality from dust. The bright gravel road, which the camper has all to itself, is bordered by a forest of diminutive trees, scarcely larger than bushes. In the fading light a dark tent city seems to extend to the distant horizon, where, as though on top of a barrier, the built-up center with its domes and towers and radio transmitters is situated. So tempting are the manifold forms of uninhabitedness that the four are determined to go there at once.

The area is not entirely deserted. A figure is standing by the roadside, signaling for a lift. The driver stops, and the hitchhiker, as nonchalantly as though getting into a bus, sits down in the back with the soldier and the old man. It is a woman swathed in a woolen headscarf, young, to judge by her eyes. The basket she props on her knees is empty, evidently she is returning home from a nearby market, where she has sold all her wares. (The only strange part of it is that she seems to have shot out of the bush, for there was no path at the place where she was standing.) Her presence underlines the feeling that this is a foreign country, but in what part of the world it is impossible to say. It could equally well be the far north or the deep south or somewhere in the interior; only the light of the particular moment lends any novelty. No attempt is made at conversation with the hitchhiker, communication seems inconceivable and undesired on either side. Only the two women have given each other appraising looks, then both turned away. The old man switches on a little overhead lamp—the light it throws on his notebook is very much like that on his lectern in the old people's home—and tries to carry on with his signs, which the bumpy ride only makes more striking and picturesque. Before each of his strokes, always consisting of a single movement, he pauses for quite some time; shut off in his immersion, he looks at nothing else. Only the soldier, sitting across from him, manages to distract his attention. He too has a book in hand; it is still closed, and he makes elaborate preparations to open it. First he holds it out, eyes it as though to determine the right distance. What he does then is not so much to open it as cautiously to unfold it. He clamps a tiny, battery-operated reading lamp to the book cover and picks up the battery in his right hand, while with his left he places over the first line of text a semi-cylindrical glass rod, which magnifies the letters and lights up the spaces between them. The lamp sheds a tent-shaped light that makes the book appear transparent. For a moment it seems as though something is happening even without the reader. But the reader, sitting there so quietly, has his hands full, moving the magnifying glass from line to line and holding the heavy battery, which he hefts like a stone. He doesn't even get around to turning the pages, the first page keeps him busy enough; each sentence takes time, and after each sentence he has to take a deep breath in preparation for the next. The reader reveals himself as a craftsman, and his dress, which only a short while before had seemed awkward on one who had long been in uniform, turns out to be right, a costume that leaves room for reading. Under the reading jacket his chest rises, his shoulders broaden, the mother-of-pearl button on his reader's shirt shimmers, and the veins in his throat swell. The reader's eyes are narrow and curve at the corners, widening at the temples as though the letters and words, though only a few inches away, form a distant horizon. These eyes show that it is not he who is digesting the book but the book that is digesting him; little by little, he is passing into the book, until—his ears have visibly flattened—he vanishes into it and becomes all book. In the book it is broad daylight and a horseman is about to ford the Rio Grande. As he watches the reader, the old man's face copies his expression. He too has become all book, almost transparent.

The mute hitchhiker has long been gone; the wrinkles in her seat have smoothed out; it is black night in the moving vehicle. Now the woman is driving, with an expression at once vigilant and faraway; beside her the gambler, sitting upright but dozing off now and then.

The old man leans forward and motions the driver to turn off. The side road, almost entirely straight, descends steeply. The bushes are so close that they lash the roof and windows. Time and again the headlights pick a torrent, with frequent foaming rapids, out of the darkness. Just once the car comes to an almost level stretch, at the beginning of which there is a wrecked sluice gate with a chain still dangling from it, and at the end—indicated by a rotting wooden wheel with a few last stumps of spokes—an abandoned mill, its windows overgrown with hazel bushes, its loading ramp heaped with torn sacks and smashed bricks, and in the shed behind it an old handcart with upraised shafts, as though ready to be pulled.

They camp for the night at the spot where the torrent flows into a river which, in moonlight of a brightness seen only in old black-and-white Westerns, appears to be deep rather than wide. A wooden bridge leads across it, and on the other side a dark slope rises abruptly. This bridge was once an important crossing, perhaps even a disputed border, for at one end of it there is still a crank for a now-vanished barrier, and the plaster around the rusted flagpole sockets is riddled with bullet holes. But at the moment the place is almost completely forsaken, especially now at night; it's not even a way station anymore; there has been only one late traveler, who was in such a hurry that he didn't even stop to look at the camper.

Now it is parked on the stubbly grass between the road and a ruined building. Nimbly, the gambler and the soldier have made up the two bunk beds without once colliding in the cramped quarters. The interior is feebly lit by invisible lamps. From a radio in one corner, which seemed at first to be turned off, a voice is heard at intervals, rattling off frequencies and place-names, many of them overseas, in international radio English. The sound can also be heard outside—where the woman and the old man are sitting by a fire. She has slipped under his cape and is resting her head on his shoulder. But here the radio is almost drowned out by the murmur of the little waterfall at the spot where the torrent flows into the river. The river itself, by comparison, seems soundless, as though it had ceased to flow.

Now all is still in the camper, and the lights are out. The fire in the grass has burned down. The woman is still sitting by the ashes, but now the gambler is there instead of the old man, at some distance from her. The woman is warming her feet in the ashes and she no longer needs a cloak. At length the gambler breaks the silence: "That battered washtub over there on the bank, big enough for a whole family, has never been a household article. During the war the partisans used it as a ferry. They would paddle it across the river at night, not here, farther up. It often capsized, and a lot of them drowned—most of them were peasants who couldn't swim; they had a secret workshop that turned out quantities of these washtubs. There's no war memorial here. Nobody even knows that this ruin was the only electrical power station for miles around; the irregular current sparked and flickered in the region's few houses, even in the farm at the tree line. The place is known only from a folk song which makes no mention of all that. It's only about the name and a love that began here." The woman has listened reluctantly, as though afraid of being lectured to; it took the key word at the end to relieve her fears; she wants no stories about places, only stories about love. The gambler takes his time, twists his ring, and says in a changed tone: "I didn't respect you then, when you were brought before us in the amphitheater; I desired you. I wanted you. Your hopelessness was so complete, your brow gave off such a radiance, that I fell in love with you. Your despair aroused me. Then, when in your calm, friendly voice you told about your way of wandering around—the professor thought it was pathological—it came to me: I've found the woman of my life, something I had only dreamed of up until then; now it had happened. A decision was possible—actually, once you appeared, the decision had been made. In your hopelessness you struck me as immaculate, pure, holy, divine, and yet you were all woman, all flesh, all body, a perfect vessel. From my seat high up in the last row, I fell on you, I penetrated you with such force and to such depth that our ecstasy rose to the point of annihilation. And in your features, though I was sitting far away, I saw no difference between the face of extreme misery, the mask of inviolable feminine beatitude, and the grimace of utter lewdness. That day we loved each other before the eyes of all, I you in your forlornness, you me in my pure compassion. Since then I have had no feeling for anyone or anything. Since that day I have had no encounter with that rarest of all things, a beautiful human being. In that hour we, you and I, publicly engendered a unique child." Whereupon the woman might have asked: "What sort of child?" And the gambler might have answered: "A child unborn to this day, perhaps already dead, perhaps unviable—a faint image, faint and becoming fainter."

The woman has listened attentively to the gambler's story. But from time to time she has shaken her head, as though the story were not to her liking, or in astonishment that such things were possible. And once she laughed, as though thinking of something entirely different. After the last sentence, she rummages in the ashes at her feet, finds a piece of wood that is still glowing, lights her cigarette with it; in the sudden glow her face is slit-eyed, masklike.

The full moon, at first yellow and huge on the horizon, is now small and white overhead, but its light is stranger than ever. Not only the whole breadth of the river glitters but also the leaves of the bushes on the banks; not only the metal parts of the camper but the wooden parts as well. The curtains are drawn, soft snores of varying pitch issue from them. Smoke rises from the ashes of the deserted campfire. In the gleaming water, a far brighter spot appears, a moving object; it crosses the river, shapeless at first, with a V-shaped glow in its wake. Mounting the bank, it shows the silhouette of an animal, too small and furry for a seal, too big and tail-heavy for an otter. The beaver crouches motionless; his eyes and ears are tiny and black as coal, his belly and feet are coated with clay. He sniffs uninterruptedly; he is the guardian of the site, he is guarding it with his sniffing. He is the master here now; he toils at night, damming the river; he has just come home from his place of work downstream.

In the morning it is summer. In the warm wind, the wall of foliage on the steep opposite bank has become a band of green, modulating from bush to bush, interrupted only in those places where the undersides of leaves shimmer pale-gray as though withered. The still half-dreaming ear mistakes the chirping of crickets for the din of cicadas. This bank as well is bathed in the light of high summer. In knee-length swimming trunks the old man stands under the little waterfall, which serves him both as shower and curtain; the woman sits with her eyes closed in a pool at his feet, quietly taking her bath, resting her head on a rock as against a bathtub; the water comes up to her chin.

The gambler and the soldier sit in the grass, playing cards. The soldier seems to be smiling, but his ears are deep-red, almost black, and oddly enough, the same is true of the gambler, who is sitting there in his shirtsleeves. The gambler shuffles, arranges his hand, plays and gathers the cards as eagerly and excitedly as if he had been a mere onlooker until then and had now at last been given a chance to play. He puts much too much energy into his movements for a friendly little game that is not even being played for money. The perspiration drips from his hair, and his shirt is plastered to his chest and back. He has taken to biting his nails when pausing to think; once or twice he tries to take back cards that he has already played—but here his opponent stops him, laying a firm hand across his fingers; and after losing he clasps his hands overhead and emits a loud curse. The woman, in a dressing gown, sits with them, applying makeup and taking it easy. The game, in which there is a winner but no winnings, has slowed all movements around it—in it they find their time measure—and, conversely, seems fenced in by slow time. What is outside the fence has lost its attraction, it frightens; there only the usual time can prevail, daily happening, history, "bad infinity," never-ending world wars great and small. There beyond the horizon deadly earnest sets in, the treetops mark a borderline beyond which the lips of those who have just died quiver in an attempt to draw one more breath; bands of men and women, outwardly using words of endearment, inwardly mute, join forces, zealots of every kind, from whom there is no escape, who move even the highest mountains into the lowlands. One would like to regard the card game as reality and, thus fenced in, remain at the peak of time. The card players sit in the grass facing each other, as though they have shed their armor and for once are showing their true faces.

The old man is the spoilsport. Suddenly he steps in, gathers up the cards, and throws them far out into the river. As though he had been absent a long time, his face is covered with stubble and sunburned. His cape, reversed, has become a bright linen sail. Wearing ankle-high shoes, a water bottle and haversack slung over his shoulder, he is equipped for a long march. On his head a bright checked woolen cap with fringed edges; in one hand an unfolded map, in the other a freshly cut hazel stick. Wearing baggy, clownlike trousers, he has thrust one leg forward and seems to be standing on one foot. Despite his violent action, he is in a cheerful mood; it's just that he has made a decision and throwing the cards away was a part of it.

After letting himself be inspected, he speaks: "The joyride is over. From here on we walk. No more riding. When people ride, there is no departure, no change of place, no sense of arrival. In a car, even when I myself was driving, I was never really traveling. My heart was never really in it. When I ride, I'm confined to a role that is contrary to my nature: in a car, that of a figure behind glass; on a bicycle, that of a handlebar holder and pedaler. Walking is the thing. Treading ground. Having my hands free. Swaying to my own rhythm. Only when absolutely necessary should one drive or be driven. Places to which I have been driven are places where I have never been. Only through walking can a place be in some measure repeated. Only through walking do spaces open up and the spaces in between sing. Only when walking do I turn with the apples on a tree. Only a walker's head grows on his shoulders. Only a walker experiences the balls of his feet. Only a walker feels a current run through his body. Only a walker perceives the tall tree in his ear—silence. Only a walker overtakes himself and comes to himself. Only a walker's thoughts have substance. We will walk. Walking is what wants to be done. And you mustn't walk like other people who, anyone can see, walk only when they have to or by accident. Walking is the freest of sports. And now it's time to get going. Places get their virtues from walkers' virtues. Oh, my undying appetite for walking, for walking out of a place and walking on forever!"

The listeners accede without protest to the old man's command. The gambler, who always has what is needed ready at hand, distributes walking equipment. The clothing is airy and the shoes, too, are light. The odd part of it is that on the four even the most ungainly garments acquire style, as though made to order for them. For all the disparity of their dress, its elegance enables them to form a group. The woman wears her headband like a tiara, the soldier his parka like a dress uniform, the gambler his dust coat like a robe of office. The last two load heavy knapsacks on each other's back, and instead of crumpling under the weight, they seem to grow, as though the extra weight were just what their shoulders needed.

The camper has been left behind deep in a shadowy thicket, where its slats gleam like a forgotten woodpile. The

forsaken spot is enlivened by a bird; its wispy legs are perched
on a stone in the middle of the brook and its longer-than-
body-length tail keeps bobbing up and down. Incessant, too,
is the sound of the water, racing over the massive round
stone, a dark, rhythmic pounding that pervades the general
roar, a sonorous vibration as of a musical instrument, or
the after-echo of a forgotten epic. The bullet holes in the
ruined building are covered by spiderwebs sprinkled with
mortar. From the bridge rises the vapor of thawing ice and
snow; the planks creak. The place has the feel of a forbidden
zone.

The walkers did not cross the bridge but followed an
old mule track along the river. We were heading downstream, but sometimes, when we looked to one side and
the waves came fast, we seemed to be moving in the opposite
direction, that is, upstream; in the end, the picture became
so reversed that we were confused—as at old Westerns,
when the stagecoach wheels appear to be moving backward.

Our first stop was at the point where the river emerged
from its valley and the bank on our side flattened out into
a plain, while the opposite slope, though still steep, re-
ceded from the bank in a long arc, leaving room beside the
water for a road, a railroad line, and finally fields, before
turning into a long mountain chain paralleling the river at
a distance.

Here, at the end of the defile, we crossed the river on
a high footbridge so narrow that we had to proceed cautiously step by step. From then on, it was a different river,
bathed in southern light, shallow, its water dispersing into
rivulets between broad banks of gravel. Sparsely inhabited;

as far as the eye could see, only an occasional lone fisherman, none of whom so much as raised his head as we hove in sight.

When we came to the road on the other side, we saw why it was unused: it had long fallen into disrepair and had never been open to ordinary traffic; it had been specially built during the world war to carry troops and supplies to the front. Grass was growing in the cracked asphalt; whole bushes and small trees had taken root, and their tops had joined to form a leafy roof. We could have walked comfortably on this straight empty road, with an elastic ribbon of moss under our feet, but our leader motioned us to the railroad embankment that ran parallel to the road.

The railroad had not by any means fallen into disuse. Trains kept passing, those heading upriver gathering speed, those heading downriver slowing down, as though approaching a considerable city—though of such a city we saw no sign. In the trains moving away from the invisible city, the passengers were sitting still, while in those approaching the station, a jolt went through the cars from first to last, ushering in a general rising from seats, and there were also repeated scenes of conductors in seven-league boots racing through the corridors from back to front. After crossing the embankment through an opening shaped like a portal, we took a gently winding path up the mountain slope, wide enough to have permitted us to walk abreast. But all of a sudden our aged leader was in a hurry and apparently wanted to be alone, so that even at the start of the climb we walked in single file. A little later the woman passed him with a cocky side glance, signifying that she no longer needed a leader, and vanished around a bend, only to reappear much later on an open stretch, silhouetted against the sky, high above her companions. Not once did she look around. Even on the shortcuts, she moved with swinging arms and head aloft, on steep hills as on level stretches. The gambler and the soldier with their knapsacks brought up the rear, walking slowly. The soldier came last, so as not to leave the gambler alone, for he was not accustomed to climbing and his knees kept buckling.

Only a short time has passed since they left the plain, and yet the very first S-curve has carried them far away: the plain's details and movements stand out clearly all the way to the snow-covered mountains on one side and the luminous mist on the other which, along with the dark ships that sail it, is called the "sea." At the same time, almost all its sounds have been swallowed up, and those few that are still audible transformed: the clanking of trains into a soft knocking, as though from behind a glass wall; and the crowing of cocks, also as from behind a glass wall, into incessant call signs. The clear, varied, quiet design is that of medieval panels, in which for the first time pure landscape became subject matter, and taken together, sea, tilled plain, and high mountains represent the whole world. The car flashing somewhere in the distance is also a part of this silent world, and despite their many different colors the houses of a settlement plunked down in a niche in the mountainside give off the same sienna tone of earth shooting up at the sky. So sharpened is the hearing by the silence here that not even the grazing of butterfly wings against the sand of the path goes unheard.

As the S-curves narrow and become more and more

overgrown with brambles, they seem to be leading nowhere, and there is reason to fear that after the next bend the path may end in an abandoned quarry and prove to be the wrong one. The boat by the roadside halfway up the slope, as thick-walled as a dugout canoe, seems to have been washed up here in prehistoric times when this upland was still covered by the sea.

After the bend, however, a first goal comes in sight: a military cemetery, as wide and deep as two or three quarries, laid out in gently rising rows—one for each letter of the alphabet. Larger than man-size marble slabs; affixed to each one a bronze tablet incised with columns of names, and over each column—unlike the names, legible even at a distance—the same word: PRESENT, in black letters which shimmer throughout this enormous field of the fallen and seem to shout from soundless throats.

The soldier takes an interest in the cemetery and examines the inscriptions, while the others regard the place as a mere way station. They take a different attitude toward the field where the dead of the defeated power lie buried. No larger than a village graveyard, it is equally overgrown with grass. Few of the wooden crosses are marked with anything but numbers; most of the names are incomplete, followed by question marks or so garbled as to suggest nicknames. Here we stop, wait for one another, drink from a water spigot, and get ready to proceed together. Next we enter a steep defile through a vault of overhanging bushes that leave the clay floor in half darkness. It is a short climb, but numerous changes occur. At first audibly gurgling, the rivulet alongside narrows after a few steps, and at the same time the muddy ground gives way to bare rock; the dividing line is reinforced by a tree root shaped like a snake. This borderline tree between brown, bricklike earth and smooth, light-colored stone is a huge, wide-branching, solitary plane tree; it shades the path, and its roots draw the last available water from the ground; in the rock which now begins there is none. Here the defile culminates in a natural staircase. After climbing the last steps side by side, the four stop close to the tip of the plane tree's uphill branch—snake-shaped like its root, thick, long, and with the bulbous head of a diamond-patterned python protruding horizontally into the air. Then, leaving the protection of the fairy-tale tree, they find themselves on the threshold of a vast plateau, at first sight so barren that the seedpod of the plane tree, swinging close to their heads, looks to them like the last token of a living world.

But for the present it is also a boon to have turned their backs forever on water and the sounds of water that have been with them so long, the roaring of the torrent, the murmur of the river, the bubbling of the spring.

The plateau slopes gently to form an immense hollow—only in dreams might one expect to see a hollow so vast—which curves upward just as gently at its distant, but clearly outlined, blue edges. The edges, as far as the eye can see, are wavy and dunelike; every single hilltop, gently sloping on the lee side and steeper to the windward, seems to ride behind the next, and all—with no mountain peak, belonging to a region yet to come, behind them—border on the open sky. Thus the plateau, an almost perfect oval extending to the horizon, seems to be a realm apart, distinct from the familiar world, not a mere region, but a country in itself, a separate continent on top of our continent.

The dominant form of this country is the oval, which spreads everything contained in it out before our eyes; between us and the horizon there seem to be no nooks and crannies, no clefts or hidden far sides of hills. All objects are seen clearly and without distortion. Thanks to the overall form, each is distinct from the others, but all are joined in a community of graceful shapes which within the oval create an illusion of active life, one might even say of frenzied expectation, as though a buoyant, festive mankind had assembled there.

Yet this country is obviously uninhabited, showing no trace of any recent civilization, such as a settlement, a sentry box, a device for measuring rainfall, or any kind of trigonometric point. The neat rows of vines in the hollow are wild juniper bushes and the great midwestern fields of yellow grain waving in the wind are one vast barren prairie. Into the prairie from all directions, almost in human form, trees

come running, withered, branchless, barkless trees, running
through pale grass. The groups of small still-living conifers,
rising at intervals from the hollow and forming a jagged line
on the upper reaches of the oval, are so bemantled in a gray
filigree of dead wood that their greenery looks like islands
in it. But what makes the country look utterly dead is its
empty sky, beneath which, when contemplated for any
length of time, the trees, even the healthy ones, take on
the aspect of ruins; for a moment it might seem that this
sky is hostile to life, so much so that the tiny bird, hardly
bigger than a fingertip, which darts out of a bush, loses no
time before squeaking with terror and diving headlong back
into its shelter. It is no doubt from such a sky that in a
prehistoric era, which in this region is still in progress, the
numerous, grotesquely shaped, bone-colored boulders,
often as big as houses, rained down, filling the whole prairie,
sprinkling the bare woods, and in places running straight
ahead like rows of megaliths, a cosmic rockfall capable of
recurring at any moment.

This chimerical country, changing shape every time
one looked at it, had a different effect on each of the four
walkers. The woman clung to the gambler, so violently as
to make him stagger, then looked back over her shoulder
in the direction of the river valley, which had long since
disappeared from view. In her panic, her face showed its
beauty: widened eyes, taut cheekbones, blood-red lips. The
gambler, ordinarily at ease under any conditions, raised his
hand to his nose—something he had done now and then
before throwing the dice or playing a card—as though to
restore his self-confidence by sniffling (he had never gam-
bled in such a country). As for the soldier, he marveled in

silence at the unknown place, delighted not to know where he was, in much the same situation as a man who wakes up far from home, not knowing where, rid of his name yet certain that he is at last *present*—for the morning, the light, the step out of doors, the raindrops in the dust, the eyes of the first person to come along, the words of the old book.

But the soldier's delight did not infect the others; for a time each of them, including the old man, the leader, remained shut up in himself; he who had been in such a hurry to reach the plateau stopped on its threshold, and the gesture with which he at first pointed out his kingdom was transformed by his lowered eyelids into an attitude of awe, discernible also in his voice, which did not find its level and was either too low or too high, too loud or too soft, as though he were constantly listening to it, as though he had never spoken an audible word in this country except possibly to himself—though obviously he had been there any number of times over the years and was thoroughly familiar with it.

"This is the place. We are there. Now we have time. This is our day, and tomorrow will be like today. Just now you are afraid, and rightly so. Here it is winter in the summertime. The clarity of this country is an optical illusion; nowhere can this wilderness be framed, ordered, and tamed by a hotel window, nowhere is there flowing water; on all sides only silence, no creature who looks at you, no one who will speak to you, no mirror image that will reassure you; under every stone there may be a viper. Here you have no opponent who will let you think out your moves, no enemy into whose eyes you can look. In this country, unlike all other places, you will not find the right moment for

anything, neither for drawing a knife nor for opening a book.
Here it will not be a case of now or never, but of always
and always! or never and never! In this country your knife
will never cut into living flesh, and here you will always be
able to read—in your books or in their commentary known
as NATURE. I threaten you and I promise you. I promise
you not only that here you will neither hunger nor thirst,
that you will have a roof over your heads and a place to
sleep, that you will return home from here—I also promise
you beauty. We shall see things in a different light; as long
as we breathe the air here, we shall perceive coherent, living
signs in all that is lifeless and confused; after the first few
steps, as long as we keep starting out in the morning and
walking in the light of this country, our inner images will
appear to us in space, in the form of a word, a rhythm, a
song, in the shaping of a story. You are new here, but not
strangers. Each of you has been here before! In the period
when you were wandering around aimlessly, you wanted to
return here, *you* traced the paths leading to this country on
the watermarks of your banknotes; when a book didn't speak
to you of this country in the daytime, your dreams spoke
of it at night. Desolate land, which for thousands of years
has served the nations only as a place of transit or a battlefield, time and again ravaged and destroyed, disparaged by
the poets who passed through, termed 'insignificant' by one
who barely turned to look and 'sea of stones' by the next—
'as though God had stood here when he cursed the earth
after the fall of man.' Without treasure vaults or pome-
granate trees, you, in your ever and ever regenerated emptiness, have always been the land of glory for our kind of

people. All my life I have been disloyal because of my accursed notebook, my tormentor here; I have been faithful to you alone, barren, devastated, inexhaustible land of pathways."

Undoubtedly, if one looked at the country as he spoke, the old man's words had the power to make things visible by giving them their contours, to raise, as it were, the lifeless hollow from the depths; but though the old man's voice rose to a quivering psalmody addressed only to the country, our group did not accept his message. The soldier listened absently, as though he knew the text in advance and was actually listening to something else; the gambler stared at the bunch of keys in his fist, from which steel points protruded between his fingers like a knuckle-duster; and the woman looked at herself in a pocket mirror which she held so close that she could only see her eyes.

With impassive features, the leader of the expedition took the mirror and threw it into the thicket; and at almost the same time he disposed of the gambler's keys and his own freshly cut hazel stick. (As though they had duplicates at home, woman and gambler didn't seem to mind.) Then he stamped his foot on the ground, bringing forth an unexpected reverberation which roused them all, including the soldier. He then called their attention to a half-buried stone slab, a fragment of a portal of indeterminate age, scraped off the lichen, strewed a handful of fine juniper needles on it, and carefully blew them over the letters, thus distributing the needles in the grooves. In this way he, as though by magic, raised a picture from the stone and, with a sweep of his magician's cape, presented it to his audience:

a weathered, ten-rayed, gnomon-less sundial scratched into the stone and made visible by the shiny brown juniper needles.

With the same air, he tore a blank page from his notebook, ripped it up, put the pieces in his mouth, chewed them in his right and left cheek by turns, took the paper pulp between his fingers, and laid it out in lines, on a second block of stone that seemed to have grown out of the ground. After giving it time to dry, he removed it and showed each one of us the imprint of the letters: DIM, which he elucidated as *"Deo Invicto Mithrae"* and translated as "To the unconquered sun god." Thereupon he pointed at the depopulated country before us, and called out his usual: "Let's get going."

This uncovering of script was what we needed. It gave us eyes for other signs of life in the wilderness: the vestiges of paving stones in the grass, the prewar milepost leaning against natural stones, the one cultivated cherry tree (in the foliage of which for a time we saw nothing, then the first glowing red fruit, and finally the sparkle and radiance that overshadowed the green of the leaves). Though the pavement soon broke off, the signs in themselves formed a kind of causeway or raised avenue, cutting straight through the wilderness as far as the most distant horizon.

The old man proceeded quickly, with lowered head and crooked shoulders; seen from behind, he gave the impression now of a dying man, now of a schoolboy. The rest of us were seized with euphoria the moment we set foot in the strange country. The woman walked on her hands and did cartwheels; the soldier and the gambler tossed a basketball, which naturally the gambler had in his knapsack, back and forth; at one stopping place they found a concrete court, belonging to an abandoned army camp, camouflaged with creepers and even equipped with a pole and a serviceable basket.

A warm sun shone in our faces. We bounded along as over a mountain meadow; what seemed to be tall prairie grass was the sparse, thin stalks which, without being trodden on, bowed under the air current raised by our steps; underneath it was dense, stubbly meadow grass. We had the feeling that we were still on a road thanks to the woven pattern of the plantains, as reliable a companion as the sparrows flying along with us from bush to bush; every time we looked there were more of them, and as they streaked through the air they took the place of telegraph wires.

Shoulders rolling, eyes fixed on the tips of his shoes, our leader was wholly taken up with his walking; his steps shook his whole body up to the bristly whorl on the crown of his head; in his preoccupation with his walking, he made one think of a blind man going his daily rounds and familiar with every bend and bump and pothole. Now he began to slow down and his shoulders grew broader. When we overtook him, he seemed entirely self-absorbed and yet on the alert, his ears wide open, receptive to the slightest bird sound or stirring of breeze. Apart from our steps there were no others far and wide.

Then his lesson began. Time and again he would stop, gather us together, and with a simple gesture call our attention one after another to the things of war and of peace, sometimes both in one. When he tapped on what looked like a woodpile, making it known to us as a wartime dugout; when he unmasked the line of brushwood zigzagging across the hollow as a trench; when he bent down and picked a handful of raspberries out of the prairie grass; when he picked up a quail's egg; when with one movement he plucked a whole bundle of herbs—a wave of fragrance, sunny-warm, and so strong that it went straight to our heads; when he pushed aside the curtain of bushes, revealing to the left of us a stone quarry that had only been deserted over the holiday and, to our right, a field of ripe corn as green as a mountain brook, its broad leaves waving in the wind; when with a wave of his arm he disclosed a treetop beheaded by lightning; when he made a golden eagle come sailing out of the empty sky and caused a streaky white cloud to grow out of the pure blue and then disappear—he was merely continuing the process begun when he conjured up the inscription.

Suddenly he broke off, forgot those around him, and pulled out his notebook, the used part of which, blackened and bloated by his entries, was as thick as an imposing volume. The barely audible sound of the CUMBERLAND pencil fell in with the other persistent sounds that intensified the silence; its rhythm was that of a Morse transmitter. The pencil spoke, interfered, argued, asked questions; it was trying to make a point. Though we could not see what was being written—the notebook was half hidden by the writer's elbow—it must have been verbs which, when we looked up after a time, had acted on the landscape. Every part of it was shot through with a soundless whirring; so that the towering of the cliffs and the lying of the savannah were as much an action as the perching of the birds in the bushes. In the grass at our feet a perpetual greening, in the sky overhead a vibrant bluing, and in between, at eye level, the forest's constantly renewed marching-across-the-plain and climbing-the-slope, all its trees, even the dead ones, as though on duty, like streetlamps advancing in long rows, their branches swinging vigorously. What *was* happened again and again in the rhythm of the pencil, and became, time and time again, what it was.

We too were seized with undirected energy. Each for himself, we swarmed out over the barren land and the tilled fields. Actually, we did nothing, we just walked. We walked singly, rapidly, strung out at a distance from one another, seldom looking toward one another, but when we did, we could be sure that our glance would be answered with an immediate wave, even by a figure at the limit of visibility; no need to shout.

The only one of us to act like a harvester was the old man. He had dropped back, as though we had no need of his leadership for the present, and kept bending over, moving back and forth as though following furrows; retracing his steps as though gleaning; spinning around or taking a few steps backward, as though to make sure of missing nothing; or from time to time just standing there, with one hand on his hip and the other shielding his eyes. When he then entered something in his notebook, he leaned into the curve as though pushing a plow around a bend. Whenever we looked in his direction, another figure was moving around the fields, not *instead of* but behind the one we had seen before, who was still walking there. In the end this one person became a miles-long procession.

When the clouds rose on the horizon, we got together again. By then we were deep in the interior; we had long been walking on the bottom of the hollow, still on the strip of prairie, which had widened until it filled the whole valley. We could tell by the clarity of the air and the light but steady contrary wind that we were still on a high plateau.

Only clouds coming from the sea can cross the horizon so quickly. In a moment they had covered the whole sky. The storm did not give the advance notice usual in inland regions: the few drops which at first only wet the stones and make them pop out of the ground in all colors, the crackling as of chirping crickets in the grass, followed by an interval of dead calm as the storm musters its forces. Here the rain broke over us unannounced, streamed down the backs of our hands, slammed into the hollows of our knees; bowing our heads, we saw sheets of water breaking over the tips of our shoes and dividing into ankle-deep rivers, through which we tried to wade. This water was heavy and increasingly cold, terrifying. Of course the gambler had a raincoat in his knapsack, large enough in fact to cover us all, but the wind had risen and the rain splattered us from the front even more violently than from above. Before long it had half blinded us and made breathing almost impossible.

In search of shelter, we headed for the bushes at the edge of the prairie, but our progress was as slow and awkward as in dreams; we kept sinking into the mud, stumbling, pulled down by the weight of our clothing, shackled at the knees, falling, stopping to catch our breath; our pursuer, instead of being behind us, was everywhere. At length we found makeshift shelter in the thicket with its roof of tough, dense-layered leaves, which reduced the watery onslaught to spray. There the four of us stayed a long while, each in a separate niche, cut off from the others by wooden bars as in individual cells, staring at the deluge which before our eyes was reducing the high plateau to a swampy, mist-shrouded plain and turning our bushes into an island.

The rain abated in fits and starts; every time it seemed to be stopping, it started up again, fortunately for shorter and shorter periods; in the end, it was falling only from a single tree in a last onslaught of the wind, which was also dying down by fits and starts. While the rain was falling, the water on the ground had been so deep that the prairie looked like a rice plantation; now, before we knew it, the water was sucked up by the soil; all that remained was a quickly receding gurgling, giving way to sounds suggesting the uncorking of bottles. The water in the bushes had dispersed into myriad drops which, instead of falling, hung from the branches in motionless chains.

There were no puddles and consequently no birds that might have bathed in them. The storm was followed by a deaf silence: the old man's word for it—he was writing again, his pencil made no sound on the dampened paper —was "nonstillness." The gray around us was not fog; it was the kind of haze, dense, uniform, without puffs or wisps, which settles on a snowy landscape when the snow has turned to rain. Our only horizon was ourselves and a few leaves, which in the dingy light looked like symbols drawn in India ink; the outermost limit of our field of vision was still within reaching distance: a black, sharply delineated, beak-shaped thorn, pointing into the unknown.

In emerging from our niches, we had to tear our clothes from the brambles in which we had unwittingly become entangled in our search for shelter. On the next leg of our journey, it was useless to look persistently at anything, as we ordinarily did. In the illusory calm, any movement, however slight, would have been noticeable; but there was none; even the bit of fluff on a blade of grass seemed to have been pasted on; even if one had blown on it, or so it seemed to us, it would not have stirred.

The wind did not start up again until late, and then from the opposite direction, as though it had turned around behind our backs. As we sensed from the start, this was an entirely different sort of wind. The former one had made itself heard by means of things—clearly distinguishable varieties of needles and leaves; the new one came on as a single undifferentiated blow, whistling and clattering like a wind that is traversing not a desert but thickly settled country whose population—just a few birds, to be sure—has sped away, all with flattened wings, lamenting like prisoners.

In no more time than it took the clouds to gather and roll away, our clothes dried; the almost inextricable knots in our shoelaces were our only reminder of the downpour. Thanks to the wind, the air had become painfully clear; whatever we looked at was too close, too sharply delineated —and deceptive to boot: side by side with trees, we saw incessant lightning flashes, their negative images; the apparent herd of antelopes that passed us by with a loud clatter of hoofbeats proved to be a single deer. The prairie grass in front of us was so thoroughly combed apart that far and wide nothing remained but the naked stone desert. This wind howled through our skulls and seemed to dominate all space; under its harrying, the moon seemed to wane, while the countryside below lay trembling, pressed into an inclined plane.

The only calm spots were behind bends in the cliff.

There, sheltered from the wind, we found ourselves in a warm, clear midsummer afternoon. In one of these oases, the soldier crouched down and pressed his fist to his forehead. The others gathered around him, looking down. At length the soldier raised his face, which had suddenly become the face of an old man. In attempting to laugh, he showed all his weakness and a moment later laughed at it without restraint. He stood up unaided, gaining new strength from the avowal of his misery. As he walked on, he moved his lips, as though preparing to say something. In reality, he was only counting his steps to himself.

Under the evening sun—long, apparently flickering shadows—our leader suddenly quickened his pace, but intimated that we could take our time. Well ahead of us, he entered a gently rising mixed forest, in the middle of which we discerned a row of cypresses that might have lined a cemetery walk. The wind was blowing so hard that the thick multiple trunks, usually cloaked in dark foliage, gaped wide in their nakedness. This was no optical illusion. At the end of the walk, the old man vanished through an arch of light, and a moment later we saw woodsmoke rising—smoke signals, we thought. Clearly, this was our goal for the day.

The old man was waiting for us at the entrance to something halfway between a natural cave and a man-made structure. Our first impression was of an ivy-clad, windowless dwelling with an ingenious door opening—on the lintel a festoon of stalactites, in the clay floor a matching threshold; between them creepers hanging like the string curtains one sees in southern countries; and a flat roof green with shrubbery. While the old man parted the strings with a

gesture of hospitality and showed us in, one of our number
automatically took off his shoes in the grass and the rest of
us did likewise. A black-and-yellow salamander, motionless,
looked up at us—the heraldic emblem of the cave hostelry.

This cave had once served as a bunker and the inner
walls had been reinforced with concrete; the stalactites hanging from the ceiling were as sooty as the meat in a smoke-
house. But this was only the vestibule; rounding a bend,
we entered another cave. Though deeper in the rock than
the first, it was lighter, thanks to a number of almost circular, seemingly artificial windows in the thin roof, where
once trees had rooted and now the outside world shone in,
its colors intensified by the windows; the entire cave seemed
irradiated by the summery green of the bushes on its roof
and their reflection in the likewise round puddles on the
floor. A plank led past the puddles into the background: a
dry "chimney corner," recognizable at a glance by the cast-
iron stove, in which the fire burst into life with a roar that
drowned out the howling of the wind (so that was why the
old man had been picking up wood on the last stretch of
the way). The stove was connected by two slanting pipes to
a hole in the wall; the thicker one served to evacuate smoke,
while the thin one carried rainwater into the reservoir of
the stove. Consonant with the picture of a hostel were the
wooden table beside the stove, the long bench against the
cave wall—whose stalactites were like smooth backrests—
and the adjoining sleeping quarters, an alcove floored with
a thick layer of foliage intertwined with corn husks and
straw, which one might have taken for mere animal litter
if not for the carefully folded gray army blankets on top of

it; an overhanging rock, this one without windows, made
the half-darkened alcove look something like a room.

This time the old man was the cook. Deftly he prepared
the evening meal from the provisions which the gambler as
usual had in his knapsack, seasoning and freshening them
with the herbs—the kernels of corn, the mountain figs and
juniper berries he had gathered on the way—which made
even canned goods tasty. The rest of us were too tired to
go out again. At first we were not even willing to get up
from the bench; while our cook washed up—that evening
left us forever with the unique image of an old, old man,
an aged innkeeper, standing high over the stove in his world-
famous kitchen, with an invisible brigade of apprentices
gathering round him—we looked out at the entrance to the
cave, where more and more leaves were blowing around
the bend leading to the bunker and coming to rest in the
quiet, or up at the window holes that had long since turned
night-black. It was a warm, wakeful weariness, in which all
of us not only heard and saw the same things but in addition
were all of the same age and sex, and had no story but the
fatigue we all had in common.

Our host hung an oil lamp on the wall and sat down
with us. The circle of light wavered at first and barely extended to our hands, which lay heavy and motionless on
the table, still swollen from our exertion; between thumb
and forefinger, as though forgotten, a last piece of bread,
a bouillon cube, a pea, a cigarette; our fingertips still shriv-
eled and drained of color from our hour in the rain, as
though our hands had been under water the whole time.
Then the wick was turned up and the light shone evenly

through the room, darkening the spaces between the stalactites on the walls and so accentuating their shapes. A
limestone surface showed the regular folds of a window
curtain drawn for the night, and the divers stalagmites rising
from the floor provided a row of sturdy but graceful household articles—jugs, bottles, cups, and bread molds.

The gambler switched on a transistor radio, so small
that it was almost invisible in his hand. We heard a fragment of the news; the speaker's voice was soft and clear,
shaping the words with excessive precision, as though ad-
dressing children or foreigners. And indeed the message was
intended for a particular group. The fragment was as follows:
". . . have been, to the best of our knowledge, no casualties.
Nor has any property damage been reported. Trains, planes,
and ships are operating normally. All the mountain passes
are open. The search parties have returned safely. Those
last reported missing are also safe and sound. The chief
cities are calm, and there have been no reports from any
part of the country of power or telephone failures. There is
no food shortage and no threat of epidemics. The steps taken
have proved effective. Since a recurrence is unlikely for the
present, no special measures are under consideration. There
has been a marked improvement in the weather . . ."

From then on the wind, which was still blowing against
the cave dwelling, and the dripping from the limestone roof
were a part of the silence. From out of this silence the voice
of our host in a tone of rising amazement: "How far we
have come today! We have traveled halfway around the
world: this morning a bone-chilling showerbath under the
waterfall; in the noonday heat the crackling bronze tablets
of the war cemetery; this afternoon battling the desert rain,

without stopping for breath, attacked from behind by the Tibetan north wind; at last, toward evening, this cave behind a cave, this kitchen—bedroom—living room around the corner from a bunker . . . How many days have elapsed for me in this one day! It took me a whole day to watch you playing cards; a second to go down the river; a third to climb up to the high plateau; a fourth to get my bearings there; then a whole week to decipher the road markings, to lead you through rain and wind to my stalactite grotto, and to make it seem as bright and hospitable to you as a mountain villa."

After a long pause, the gambler spoke: "My parents have long been dead. But each imprinted an unmistakable image on my memory. Though I probably saw them many a time afterward, I feel as though those images were their last. I see my mother weighed down with shopping bags, climbing a steep hill on her way home. She is alone—there's no one in sight far and wide—dragging herself laboriously up the hill, and it's not just because of her bags. She doesn't notice me at first; her face is strange, a man's face. For the first time I see her as she is. As she is? Forsaken, cast out of the human community, aching with loneliness; before her eyes, unblinking in spite of the sun, death. And her expression doesn't change when she sees me; she shows neither surprise nor pleasure; she doesn't *want* to dissemble now, that's her strength. With the strength of her despair, she aims a short contemptuous glance at the person who, for all she cares, can come to meet her until the end of time but still won't be her child. Already she has passed him without a word. My father is sitting in a small clearing, deep in the woods, where the two of us have gone to pick blueberries. He is sitting in the grass at the junction of several paths, leaning with outstretched legs against a wooden cross. Though he is a practiced walker and still relatively young, he is suddenly too tired to go on. He doesn't want me to stay with him, he tells me to go picking alone. Lying there with his hands on his belly, he really seems to be pleading when he says: Please go; and the look in his eyes expresses not only pain but acquittal and release. I may be dead tired—but never mind, leave me, my boy; I, your father, will stay here awhile and wait for you. In these two images, my parents are still alive for me. Whenever I come to that steep path, in reality or in my thoughts, my mother comes plodding along, looking through me in her saintly despair, and whenever I pass that grass triangle in the middle of the woods, I see my exhausted father watching me over his shoulder. But today I need neither that particular path nor that particular clearing; wherever I've been, my mother or my father has been there, too. Detaching themselves from those two memories, they come to me in the air, figments of light, consisting solely of glances. In today's desert world, more than ever before, I have felt myself seen and observed by my parents. And the glances did not come only from my parents—all my fore-bears were there, watching me as I passed through the empty country; a whole far-flung clan, totally unknown to me before, has been looking at me. I too have the feeling that in this one day I have experienced several different days, so varied have been their looks, looks of horror turning to amazement, turning to indulgence, turning to approval, turning to understanding, turning to solidarity—until at the end of the long day the glance of my forebears was one with

mine and fused into something else, a voice which at last
has made it possible for me to mourn my father and mother,
and also, for the first time in the fifty years of my life, bade
me welcome on earth, while at the same time calling out
to me, bidding me think about someone else, care for him,
do something for him, do everything for him, this minute.
Now! I would like to be on the move like this as long as I
live."

While the gambler was speaking, the soldier had picked
up a handful of alabaster-white stones no larger than peas,
which in times gone by had been pebbles at the bottom of
a brook and in other bygone times had fallen from aerial
tree roots. He passed them rhythmically from hand to hand;
the sound was now as of marbles, now as of a distant hail-
storm, now as of shots, and now as of old coins. Though
he hadn't said a word all day, he had no need to clear his
throat before speaking: "When I was a child, I could see a
plain from our window. It was a large plain, all fields and
meadows. I wished it were full of houses all the way to the
horizon, white, modern houses with flat roofs. I wanted our
village to become a big city. Day after day, I looked out
impatiently, to see if they hadn't started building somewhere; the few wooden farm shacks didn't count. When at
last would the name of our village be known throughout
the world like Buenos Aires or Hokkaido or Vladivostok or
Santa Fe? My wish has almost come true. The village has
not become a city, but the plain is covered with housing
developments named after the former owners of the land,
and all look equally suburban. 'North,' 'South,' 'East,' or
'West' has been added to the name of the village and that
makes the scattered developments sound like sections of a

city; there's even a peripheral highway and a feeder road leading to the expressway, where the traffic roars just as it did in my childhood visions. A toolshed has become a telephone booth, still roofed over by the same arching elder bush. Beside the roadside shrine stands the kiosk I longed for, with stationery, newspapers, and even a few books for sale. Only in the pictures my father paints is the plain as empty as in my childhood. He says he works from nature; every morning he sets up his easel in front of some new building, but what appears on his canvas is always the empty landscape. He says all he needs is a little space here and there between the houses; in those small gaps the old open spaces burgeon, and he has only to transfer them to his canvas; he says the paint he uses is like that bacillus which dissolves otherwise indestructible things into air. Which reminds me of another, very different idea I had in my childhood: when I walked across country in those days, I was convinced that the stones in the fields were growing just like the grass and the grain, and that in time they'd get to be as big as houses. I didn't think of them as having roots; I endowed them with an inner force and regarded them, unlike the plants, as living beings. I was sure that if I measured them, they would become appreciably larger from measurement to measurement. All day today I've been thinking through my father's pictures, step by step and degree by degree, as in a circle: the cliffs in this country have taken the place of my big-city houses. It's only my father that I miss. I've never missed him as much as here. Father, I miss you. I've always missed you, I'll miss you until I die: I miss you because you despised my suffering; I miss you as my authority, my storyteller, my withholder; I miss you as a home, as the hand on my head in dreams, as a smell, as my soul; I miss you to the point of blindness, enough to make me pull a knife, to make me scream. Father, appear!" This last word had been shouted. Knife in hand, the soldier jumped up from the bench. But instead of throwing the knife, he threw pebbles, which rained down on the rock. Outside, the upland stars flickered as though twisted by the wind. A wild boar was a motionless hump in the underbrush; some smaller humps lay beside it. A cornfield with its glittering, waving leaves counterfeited the moving surface of a lake; the handcart alongside it played the part of a boat. The curving glow over the undulating, always identically distant horizon rose from the big seaport at the foot of the plateau; it was as though the soldier's shout had landed there and the glow was its echo.

Much later, as we were all lying on our bed of foliage, the woman spoke. The oil lamp had been turned low, and the room lay in half darkness. As we were lying prone, our heads to one side and our hands over our eyes, it was impossible to tell who was awake and who was asleep. Only the woman was visible, lying with her eyes closed and her face framed and half buried in her pillow of foliage, as children sometimes do in their autumn games. And so clear was her toneless voice that, again as with children, it would have been hard to say whether she was talking in her sleep or pretending. On her couch, which was somewhat higher than the others, she lay as on a royal bed, and with her under it the army blanket lost its military look. This is what she said: "You're a liar. You've deceived me from the first. You've never meant what you said. You're a cheat, a con

man, a swindler. You lured me into a trap. If I go to the
dogs, you're to blame and you should be punished for it.
DIM is not an unconquered sun god, it's a brand of panty-
hose. You're a rotten reader. You say: I like to be disturbed;
the truth is, you can only be alone, and not just with
yourself, no, you've got to be alone with your books, your
gold pencils, and your stones. Your supposed sundial wasn't
scratched on the rock centuries ago by some great man, but
only yesterday by a child at play, and it's not a sundial, it's
just a scribble. You're a phony scholar. There's no inspi-
ration at the bottom of your reading, deciphering, and
interpreting—they're just a quirk; you invented the voice
that said to you: Take this and read; ever since you've been
able to see, you've been obsessed with your written word,
your letters, your signs. Your Roman milepost was a prop
left here by some filmmakers. Same with your oldest inscriptions, they came from a movie set. Tap your bronze
—it sounds hollow; run your fingernail over your runes—
the cardboard will squeak. Your Egyptian scarab was man-
ufactured last year in Murano, and the flower on your
fragment of a Cretan vase was etched in Hong Kong. And
even if they are authentic, what they have to say is old stuff
and signifies nothing today. Their meaning is lost, their
relevance forgotten, their context broken off. Far from re-
capturing the thread, we can't even get an inkling of it.
Only your words on your false and authentic stones remain,
and they have been drowned out not only by the thunder
of war machines but by the fall of the very first empire.
Never again will your Euphrates and your Tigris flow from
Paradise. Never again will your child carried across the sea
by a dolphin serve as a symbol of solace on the graves of

those who die young. In none of your books will there be
another Odysseus, another Queen of Sheba, another Mar-
cellus. You yourself no longer believe in the fords you've
shown me. Your springs mean no more to you than they
do to me; your crossroads and clearings have long ceased
to be special places for you; at your watersheds you stand
bewildered like any other tourist—what good does it do you
to know that the water from one of the twin pipes flows into
the Baltic and from the other into the Black Sea? And for
years your country here hasn't been to you what it once
was. The emptiness here no longer promises you anything;
the silence here has ceased to tell you anything; your walking
here has lost its effect; the present here, which once seemed
so pure and uniquely luminous to you, darkens between
your steps as it does anywhere else. Here, too, empty has
become empty, dead dead, the past irrevocable, and there
is nothing more to hand down. You should have stayed
alone in your room. Out of the sun, curtain drawn, artificial
light, easy chair, television, no more adventures or distrac-
tions, gaze straight ahead, no more looking for inscriptions
out of the corner of your eye, no more glancing over your
shoulder into dark recesses, no more turning about, no more
prayer, no more talk; only silence, without you. It would
be so lovely there now, without you, in an entirely different
prairie from yours. *Vanity Fair! Vogue! Amica! Harper's
Bazaar!"* While she was speaking, the wind had slackened,
and by the time she finished, it had died down completely.
In the upper window openings the night sky had come
closer; the veil hanging from a branch was the Milky Way.
The four sleepers lay in different directions, as though
dropped at random. The gambler's hand above the blanket

took the woman's hand under the blanket, and so their hands rested. Suddenly the sleeping woman cried out with pain; her breath caught, then came a sob that shook her whole body, and tears streamed from her closed eyes. In her dream she saw a man who had just died, and that made her the last human being in the world. She cowered on the ground, and all she had left was a childlike whimpering, stopping and starting up again each time on a higher note, filling the room but heard by no one.

The countryside is utterly silent. The cave dwelling takes on steel edges in the dawning light. The mounds of bat droppings on the floor of the bunker are shaped like sleeping bags. No more smoke above the chimney hole; no dew in the grass; certain stones have holes in them like animal skulls, the sky enclosed in them is a grayer, more ancient stone. The old man with the canvas-covered book has stepped out into the open; wet as though newly washed, his hair shows its length. He combs it without a mirror, looking inward. Instead of his cape, he is wearing a wide shirt; hanging down over his belt and buttoned askew, it is well suited to his clown's trousers; but the creases are sharp, as though he were wearing it for the first time.

He walks quickly, at first swinging his notebook like a discus, then tucking it into his trousers and drumming on it to the rhythm of his steps. The drumming sounds hollow and soon fills the wilderness; little by little the details of the landscape emerge from the gloom and take on contours.

Later, when, glancing over his shoulder, he sees the cave dwelling as nothing more than a rock among many others, the old man begins to sing. He has long since changed direction—what started out as an open plateau has acquired steep walls on all sides. Now he is roaming through a jungle almost all of whose trees are dead—roaming happily, as though triumphing every time he stumbles. He has kept on writing, but now he does it while walking, no longer in his book but in the air, drawing big letters. In a hoarse falsetto voice he sings:

Into the silence.
Alone into silence.
Silence alone.
Where are you, silence?

You've always been good to me, silence.
I've always been happy in you, silence.
Time and again, I've become a child with you, silence;
through you I came into the world, silence;
in you I learned to hear, silence;
from you I acquired a soul, silence;
by you alone have I let myself be taught, silence;
from you alone have I gone as a man among men, silence.

Be to me again what you were, silence.
Embrace me, silence.
Take me under the armpits, silence.
Make me silent, silence;
and make me receptive, silence—
only receptive, silence.
I cry out to you, silence.
You above all, silence.

Silence, source of images.
Silence, great image.
Silence, imagination's mother.

In the first stage of his wanderings, the old man had seemed to be deliberately leaving a trail, bending branches to the left and right of his path, letting thorns pluck threads from his shirt and fluff from his trousers, and making an oblique scratch on every boulder with his steel comb. But then, falling silent, he not only stopped blazing a trail but at a certain point retraced his steps and erased his last scratch, which thus became a natural crack in the stone.

At first he had followed animal tracks through the prairie grass; now he avoided them. It was through a kind of maquis with increasingly narrow passages between bushes that he twined his way without hesitation.

He kept going until his shoelace came loose. He bent over to tie it and then sat down, as though he had been waiting for just this. He had come to a place where the thicket opened up into an almost circular clearing, a patch of sandy desert in the middle of the high plateau; the more than ankle-deep sand had long ago been blown into hard ridges, but below the surface it was soft and warm from the sun of the day before. The old man took off his shoes and buried his bare feet in it.

This desert, no larger than a children's playground, was not old; a single plant was growing in it, tall, shaggy, half tree, half bush, threaded with dead plants of various kinds that made it hard to identify. There were signs of fruitfulness in the thornbushes around it—blackberries and thirst-quenching anise stems.

With these the old man rounded out his breakfast—a crust of bread taken from his trouser pocket. In the morning sunlight the tip of the withered tree over his head seemed to have put on fresh green. Deep within the cagelike network of branches, the black silhouette of a bird, also of indeterminate species, motionless, but with head and tail upraised.

Nor was the sky entirely empty. A plane was crossing it, so high, so soundless, so slow, and so white that it could be seen literally as an airship.

The old man reached for his notebook, which lay beside him in the sand, hesitated, and said in a voice from which the last assurance, born of his wandering, had vanished: "Heart, now you are alone with me. At least, as I have always wished, this is happening to me in a foreign country. How long is it since someone put his arm over my shoulder and said: You can't just write all year long; and how long since someone else said about me: Always reading. From the start I have been incapable of applying the great fundamental law that I read in nature to my life and transmitting it to my fellow men—I have succeeded in applying it only to my writing and only when alone. Only when I was alone did things take on meaning for me, and only the signs I discovered when alone have been communicated to others. And now my writing time is over. My longing is dead. I know it, I know its place in my heart; it's there, but dead. So where can I go now? And where am I? Do places exist no longer? Have I burned up all the light inside me? Can't I look forward to beauty any longer? Am I then lost? Is it all up with me? Or am I, in my weakness, at my goal?"

He arose from the sand and walked back and forth in the patch of desert; suddenly his legs became short and at each turn his shoulders grew broader. He described wider and wider loops around the dead tree with the almost invisible bird in it. Now and then it gave forth a rustling sound. Otherwise there was no sign of life nearby; even the one ant trail was deserted, and the holes in the ground were empty.

He sat down again with his book, and rested his forehead on it. His eyes narrowed, taking on the shape of two dugout canoes. The silhouette of the bird, still motionless, beak and tail upraised, suggested a fairy tale. Suddenly, as though of its own accord, the familiar sound of the pencil set in, followed by a persistent scraping. The hand with the brownish liver spots wrote in the notebook on the old man's knees. The writer did not look at the paper but kept his eyes fixed straight ahead. Then the movements of his hand slowed down as though for fear of frightening the bird away, and in the end he seemed to be drawing rather than writing.

The silhouette is gone from the thicket. In place of the bird a cloud of sand blows down, making the dry wood crackle. And of the old man nothing remains but the imprint of his behind. In his absence the blackberries glisten and whitish-yellow umbels blossom at the edge of the desert. The parched soil in which they are rooted shows a polygonal pattern of finger's-breadth cracks. An airplane in the summer sky sounds as if it were hovering motionless.

When the others awoke, their eyes fell on a spot of sunlight on the gray wall of their cave. In it, the otherwise dull-white sinter shone bottle-green as though dripping wet, and although this small bright spot had no particular shape, the moment we all of us at once opened our eyes, it spoke to us with the authority of a sign: Arise! It is day, everything is here; out with you, into the open; bestir yourselves.

None of us felt the usual grogginess, we came to our senses immediately; we knew where we were and arose lightheartedly from our nightmares, looking forward with rare delight to the morning. The spot on the wall seemed to make us inventive. Without even looking, we found among the numerous puddles on the ground a deep one from which to gather water for washing and making coffee.

We ate breakfast in the grass outside the bunker. The plateau, rising steadily like a ramp as far as the horizon, lay there in the sun as though contemptuous of the four seasons. It seemed hardly imaginable that there could be any life apart from these trees and these few birds. Yet beyond "extensive scree," "dry ditch," "stony riverbed," "bald hill," our leader's map noted a "lake" (with "landing") and near the landing a "log cabin," from which a hatched-in path led to an "old road" (a line), soon prolonged by a "new road" (two parallel lines) beginning at a nameless "village" and ending at an equally nameless "city." In view of the actual country confronting us, the old man's map, with its pedantically delineated cliffs and even individual trees, put us in mind of the early fantastic topographies that represented the most inhospitable terrain as accessible and made it seem likely that a whole continent could be crossed on foot in a single day.

We assumed that the old man had gone on ahead of us, that he had left the map to enable us to follow him, and would be waiting for us somewhere along the way, at the latest that evening in the city. A light, steady breeze blew in our faces from the start—hadn't that breeze been raised by his steps? Surely it was so fragrant because of the herbs he carried—mixed, concentrated, and warmed—in his trouser pockets. If we had called him, it wouldn't have been out of worry but out of playfulness—yes, but by what name?

All day we walked with the thirst for knowledge that had taken hold of us in our moment of waking. Though supposedly there was nothing more to investigate or discover on earth, we approached every new landscape with the eagerness of explorers, and circled each object in a collective joy of discovery. Our perception was never purely external; it was always an assimilation, which engraved colors, forms, and relationships indelibly on our minds and strengthened us; we never so much as thought of appropriating, but saw things as values in themselves; their mere presence made us feel that we had recovered from something. We wanted only to embrace them, feel them, measure them, and transmit them; didn't even the most unassuming blade of grass deserve to be noticed and communicated—at least with a faint cry? Our day of discovery brought us news that obviated the need for any conceivable newspaper.

That day nothing could happen to us. Of the snakes in the rubble we saw only the dark tips of their tails as they disappeared between stones, and the gambler, despite his lack of exercise, proved unexpectedly nimble in jumping from boulder to boulder. The woman, with the old man's cape over her shoulders, danced as surefooted as in a dream through the rocks and stumps that encumbered the dazzlingly white riverbed. And when the soldier, racing up to the bare hilltop ahead of us with the knapsack bobbing up and down on his back like a child's schoolbag, staggered and fell as though shot, he was merely acting out a scene from his past.

Instead of pausing at the summit, we descended directly to the lake; in addition to walking and jumping and climbing that day, we kept *arriving*. At first sight the lake was only a pale-yellow forest of reeds. At its edge we found a boat, chained to a tree. The view from above had shown us that the other side could be reached most easily on foot; but we followed our scout's directions and took the boat, though we first had to bail it out and then use our hands as paddles. The unusual things about this small lake were the trees half submerged in it and the clear water that rose in visible whirls from the stony bottom. The woman soon left the paddling to the others, draped herself in the cape, and stood erect in the bow. Though the breeze was barely perceptible, the leaves of the tall alders all around the lake rustled incessantly, and the rustling grew louder and louder, more and more tempestuous, until it seemed to do away with every other sound; no waterfowl screamed and no fish leapt out of the water. When in the apparent jungle on the far shore we saw a signboard—the first indication of human presence in a long while—were we relieved? Weren't we equally disappointed?

On landing, we found that the sign was rusted through and barely legible; we finally deciphered BEWARE—HORNETS; to judge by the style of lettering, the sign dated from before the war. The dock, too, was rotten; the remaining piles were crooked, some driven more deeply than others, and overgrown with moss; in addition, the dock was well out of the water, because the lake had shrunk considerably over the years. The dead willow trees had great holes in them; the moss line on their trunks indicated the former water level.

Our first sign of the present time was the "log cabin."
This was a café with its own adjacent generator, which—
CLOSED FOR THE DAY—was not working just then. In the
dim light behind the large glass window we saw a bar and
behind it a fireplace piled with logs ready to be lit. Outside,
among scattered garden benches, there was a table-soccer
game; in passing, we turned the knobs, and when we left,
all the little wooden men had their feet in the air.

Although the path shown on the map proved to be a
wide grass walk and we had plenty of room to spread out,
we stayed as close together as we had been in the boat. The
slightly raised green path was springy; from time to time the
woman would take the soldier by the wrist and the two of
them would dance along in wide spirals, while the gambler,
smiling, brought up the rear. For a while it was possible to
imagine that this was a region offering an escape from history, yet at the same time a new country where something
might be begun.

On the "old road," which our descending path suddenly joined, the plateau reverted to stone-gray. Though
the gravel surface seemed well kept and even new, we saw
no trace of any vehicle, nor was there any dust on the
bushes. As sudden as the transition from green walk to desert
track was the change from sea air to heat unstirred by any
breeze. For hours we were directly under the sun, as in an
everlasting noon. Outlook there was none; the road, straight
on the map, rose and fell at such short intervals that there
was never a distant horizon. The few clouds, somber with
bright edges, remained motionless, grouped together in a
sea-blue sky like a cluster of islands seen from a space capsule
high overhead: the Sporades. The abundant blackberries by

the sides of the road brought no refreshment; a whole handful slaked our thirst for hardly the time it took to swallow
them. The silence in which we had been at home up until
then degenerated into soundlessness; even the soft familiar
hum of the crickets was gone—at our approach, their black
heads disappeared into holes in the ground; the only sound
apart from our own was that of the grasshoppers darting
from under our toes.

Suddenly, like everything that happened in this high
country, a crackling and whirring as of rain came from
above, though the sky was still bright. The road narrowed
and became a mere passage through head-high underbrush,
which on one side had the appearance of a hedge purposely
planted there. Here the old road met the "new" one, but
did not merge with it; the two ran parallel for a short way,
then the old road, now no wider than a smuggler's trail,
lost itself in the prairie grass. A hare appeared, sniffed the
air, and vanished. The sound of rain came from a power
line; no sooner had we climbed the embankment than its
wires, leaping from otherwise empty space beyond the new
road, came so close to us that for a few steps their crackling
was a downpour.

Narrow and winding, the road was more like a track,
but a sturdy one, built for the centuries, as though it were
the only thoroughfare in the land, comparable to a segment
of the Silk Road or the Pan-American Highway. Surfaced
with neither gravel nor asphalt, it was a stone track which
its builders had developed into a road merely by scraping
the layer of humus off the rocky base, as the shoulders,
barely a foot wide, indicated. This natural road was com-
pact, without cracks, and so smooth from the very start that

there was no need to roll it; the few bumps had been worn down. Who but ourselves had traveled this road in recent years? Perhaps a few vehicles, covered wagons laden with heavy sacks, barrels, and emigrants. (In spite of ourselves, we kept looking back over our shoulders for the next trek.)

The steady rise of the road encouraged us and made us breathe deeply. Because of the many bends, there was still no outlook; we were confident that the country would open out at any minute. No road marker, no indication of distances. Only the dead butterflies stuck to the ground here and there and the spots of oil showed that this was a motor road. Certain that we were alone on it, we walked side by side until, on rounding a curve, we saw a handcart parked in a recess in the rock and automatically stepped aside, as though it were coming toward us. The impression made by the presence of this cart in our no-man's-land was strangely contradictory; on the one hand, it suggested that the familiar rhythm of time had caught up with us only too soon—we ought to have stuck it out a lot longer in the land of uncertainty and explored it; on the other hand, those two wheels in the otherwise total wilderness struck us as amazing inventions, made in that moment and thanks to us!

Then suddenly the landscape became a battlefield. On both sides of the road tanks appeared, their guns apparently aimed at us. From every opening, fire and thunder shot out in our direction. Soldiers laden with clanking metal came charging through the bushes. An observation tower glittered with binoculars. No more bird sounds.

After the next bend our eyes fell just as suddenly, in the midst of the long row of natural caves, on an improved cave dwelling, recognizable by the wooden props at the entrance and the barred gate. On the clay floor lay not stones but a great heap of potatoes. In front of us we saw, instead of the expected field, a stand of spruces, young trees that seemed freshly planted, their dark-green tips in serried regular lines. The road that led through them, straight and unexpectedly wide, appeared to be a farm or a forest path. Again our delight in all this warred with our distress at being back so soon in familiar Central European surroundings. We were therefore well pleased when suddenly, after the reforestation, we found ourselves surrounded by prairie grass, and out of the corners of our eyes we saw the mirage of a wheat field. In this phase, such optical illusions became more and more frequent, and in the end we saw nothing else. The cause of this, more than fatigue, was our searing thirst, which dulled our senses and scorched our mouths and throats. In vain we waited for the gambler, who ordinarily had something handy for every emergency, to conjure up some liquid; one great desert extended from our throats to the horizon.

Were we on the wrong road? Had we in our half blindness overlooked a turnoff? We were immensely relieved when on a last curve, after which the road opened out into a plain that might have been the very roof of the high plateau, we suddenly saw a human form far ahead of us. We broke into a run; our shadows on the crevice in the rocks quivered like torches. The figure ahead of us, clothed in bright colors, swinging not only his roundish head and his shoulders but his whole body, could only be our old man. We would have shouted if thirst hadn't extinguished our voices. We had to get closer before we realized that he was not coming toward us as we had thought at first but moving in the same direction as ourselves; and closer still before it became clear to us that the supposed old man was a child with a schoolbag on his back. But we had not yet caught up with him when a large, shiny, new bus that we hadn't heard coming emerged from a side road, picked up the child, and after a short straight stretch on the highway turned off into another side road with a loud blowing of its horn, as though gathering up children dispersed in this wild country. The next person we saw really was an old man, and even from fairly close up we took him for ours. Almost invisible behind the standing grain, he lay sleeping on the roots of a lone tree a short way from the road.

For the first time that day we halted for a short moment. Our instant image of our old man was composed from the hand on the ear, the blissfully idiotic dreamer's face, and in particular the hazel stick leaning against the tree trunk —but even before one of us shook him awake, that image had succumbed to the reality of a sleeping farm worker in an apron, with a straw hat on the back of his head, and blackened, cracked-claw-like arthritic fingers, which could no longer have wielded a sickle, let alone a pencil.

The sleeper's place of work seemed to be a garden, fenced off from the prairie, all by itself without a house. There must have been a water spigot somewhere, for a hose came snaking through the tall grass and ended among the garden beds. The crops—the tomatoes and currants, for instance—had been harvested or else were of such a variety that the mere sight of them only added to our thirst: onions, garlic, and artichokes that might have been mistaken for thistles. Following the hose, we came to a long stone wall, beyond which the colorless prairie changed without transition to a light-green field of short grass; and the rock in the middle of it proved to be the work of human hands, in other words, a house. Presenting a sweeping curve along the road, its untrimmed stone and few porthole-like windows caused it to resemble a small fort, in any case a military installation of some sort; from a number of fires in the grass, all abandoned, smoke rose into the sky, so dense, straight, and sharply outlined that we really thought: pillars. The voices that came out to us also fitted in with the notion of a military installation, as though the rooms were enormous and almost empty. But when we approached the long wall, it proved to be the street front of the "village" marked on the map. It consisted of a single wide façade without demarcations between the houses. Of these there were more than a dozen, but this we found out only by looking through one window after another. Behind each window there were apartments with separate entrances and—on the far side— windows through which we saw arbors, flower gardens, and, lined up in depth, the back yards of inns. Here, each of us at a window, we were given water, each in a different kind of pitcher or jug—only the lemon we were each handed was the same. We drank and drank and drank; not until it came time to take our leave were we capable of speaking. None of us had ever exchanged such natural greetings, and for the time it took to say those few words, it seemed conceivable that the human language had originated in the need for such greetings and the pleasure they conferred.

Our thirst slaked, we had new eyes for distances. As we went on, we saw the ridge of the plateau's roof; it seemed weighed down and crowned by a mass of gigantic cube-shaped boulders. Toward evening a fluorescent brilliance flared up in one of the boulders and immediately afterward —there! there! there!—another and another, until the cliffs on the horizon proved to be a city. When we stopped on the road, we were overtaken by a slow-moving patrol car, barely large enough for a single policeman, who lowered his window and looked us over. Was it the special sort of look the young soldier gave him in return that made the policeman just nod and accelerate—a look that disarmed by placing a peaceful image between itself and the world and infusing light even into repellent ugliness?

And again, as though in response to the soldier's look, a bus stopped on the open road and let us get in. Was it the same bus as before, which had by then completed its circuits in the backcountry? If so, it had let the child off somewhere and picked up no other passengers. But were we "passengers"? We were alone in the bus, in seats high above the road; behind us there were small cars, none of which passed us. Little by little we became a convoy. Apparently we were being escorted to the city with a police car in the lead. And sitting erect with our hands on our knees, looking straight ahead, we found this perfectly natural.

The city had no suburbs. A moment before in the paling light we had been passing country walls that gave the effect not only of being dilapidated but of having suddenly caved in. Already the road was ending and we were outside the railroad station. Was the whole city just an extension of the station? What other buildings were there apart from the offices of the railroad administration? In any case, only their façades were floodlit, and otherwise there was no street

lighting. The revolving sign that flickered above the roofs
in the twilight turned out to be moving trains. Proceeding
on foot, we found other hallmarks of a city, such as a park
and a movie house. There was no fountain in the park—
a ring of palm trees around a cedar—and the movie house,
like the country walls, had been reduced to a ruin, this
obviously with great suddenness—clean cracks such as the
passage of time alone does not produce; the ticket office had
collapsed, and the clock on top of it, dial, glass, and mech-
anism, was a total wreck. The earthquake must have taken
place a long time ago, the faces on the once-colored posters
were all beyond recognition. The houses that followed were
new, built of thick, undressed concrete. Suddenly the dark
city seemed full of life, because the passersby were a mixture
of all races, and there was no way of knowing whether these
constantly moving people, foreigners like ourselves, none
with eyes for anyone else, were fugitives or whether, each
for himself, they were on their way to some feast.

Standing in the middle of the sidewalkless street, a
doorman motioned us into his hotel with a sweeping gesture.
As with the bus driver before him, we took him for an agent
of our old man. The lobby was resplendent, as though
brand-new; we were the only guests. The one and only
attendant let us pick our own rooms, which were in every
way alike, all decorated with pictures of the city before the
catastrophe and the day after it.

Bathed and changed, we repaired to the dining room,
which, like the whole hotel, was empty and brightly lit. A
man's voice, chanting in a cracked singsong to the accompaniment of a harpsichord, was issuing from the loudspeaker. Listening in the doorway, we assumed it to be the

voice of our old man, and when seated we looked for him under the disguise of the waiter, previously the receptionist. Wasn't his hair dyed? Hadn't the liver spots on the backs of his hands been burned off? Weren't the lenses of his glasses mere window glass? In the end we asked him for some information just to see his pencil and his handwriting. Dissemble if you will, your monogram imprinted in the sand of the cigarette urn in the entrance is trace enough for us.

Though we were alone in the room, the festive illumination, the trailing plants along the walls, and the bay trees that flanked the tables gave us the feeling that we were surrounded by invisible people. Every time the waiter came through the swinging door with his brass, dome-shaped cart —revealing a kitchen so glaringly white as to efface any figures that may have been there—he was followed by cries and a hubbub of busy voices, as though this were a moment of feverish activity. We were sure that when the meal was over the old man would appear in the doorway in a chef's hat and receive our applause, smiling bashfully, with the modesty characteristic of master chefs.

Suddenly the hall was full of diners; additional waiters hurried in from all directions; evidently people kept late dinner hours in this town; and though we had seen only foreigners in the streets, all these late diners seemed as casual as only natives can be.

Each time we looked up in vain, our hope waned a little; each time we mistook someone for the Awaited One, our memory of the man himself grew dimmer. Did he really exist? Weren't he, his pencil, and his notebook mere delusions? And who were we—the woman with the pursed lips, the young fellow with the dirty fingernails, the unknown man with the pimp's bracelet and the corresponding bundle of banknotes?

When did the thought come to us, all of us at once, that the missing man had vanished forever? It happened suddenly in the dining room that was once again empty— the waiters had left long ago; the festive illumination and harpsichord music were unchanged, but the singing voice was gone. A thought without an image, accompanied by a nausea that made us speechless, incapable of so much as an outcry. Each for himself, without a parting word, by separate itineraries—elevator, stairs, service entrance—we went to our separate rooms, followed by the music, which resounded through the corridors, that music of which the poet said that heard in the distance it filled all those with horror who knew that they would never return home.

All night long the city seemed to be one vast railroad station: in all the rooms shunting sounds were heard, interspersed with loudspeaker voices calling out strings of place-names such as "Venice-Milan-Ventimiglia-Lyon-Paris," or "Istanbul-Salonika-Belgrade-Zagreb-Munich-Ostend," and it seemed to us that these resonant litanies intensified the effect of the music. The only other sounds were strangely tinny bells and an occasional whimpering and howling nearby, so wild that one of us thought of a madhouse, one of a prison, and one of a zoo. But never a barking, not even in the distance, as though, perhaps since the earthquake, there was not a single dog in the whole city.

But to make up for it, the cocks started crowing in the

early darkness, so many in so many different places that we thought we were out of doors and that hotel and city were an illusion. Our only certainty was that something had happened to the old man, and that certainty, instead of calming us, made us see ghosts. Didn't people who had just died—especially those who had been dear to one in life— become terrifying revenants if one hadn't taken leave of them properly?

So then the old man went into the phase of evil absence. And it persisted. He lurked in the darkest corners of the room and attacked us in our instant-long insomniac dreams; and in the morning sun he was still there, ready to pounce. At the very same moment, one of us screamed because he had seen the old man's cape on a clothes hanger, one recoiled from the glove on the balcony railing, while one pulled his knife and spun around because he had mistaken his own hair, hanging down over his face, for a marauder. The "dead man" had become a multitude of dead men, and all had banded together against us forlorn survivors.

Breakfast was served us on the terrace overlooking the hotel park. Though seated at the same table, we were not in any sense "together." We were strangers to one another, more so than the night before. Shoulder to shoulder, we seemed to have partitions between us. Had we ever had anything in common? Stupid mishap, falling in with these particular people! Stupid illusion of kinship that has sent me and these people to this weird place.

Worse than estrangement, there was hostility between us. None of us found the strength to go his separate way or to content himself with staying there, looking around him and playing with his thoughts. Glued to the spot, unable to take an interest in anything, we were enemies and would soon come to blows. The woman kept crumpling slips of paper and setting fire to them, as though burning us in effigy. The gambler shivered in the balmy air and at intervals exploded in suicidal laughter, as though about to run amok. Even the mild-mannered soldier, staring at always the same line in his book, incapable of reading, red in the face, bared his teeth from time to time. Losing each other's contours, we were no longer face to face; we did what we had never done before—we judged, deprecated, and in the end hated one another.

It was a clear, cloudless day in the early fall, with a breeze such as one might imagine on an atoll in the South Seas. The whole plateau unfolded before us; in our normal state of mind every rise and fall in our journey would have come alive for us; with a sense of being young that we would never have had without our journey, we would have seen ourselves as human clouds, advancing from station to station, resting, sleeping, indestructible. We would have delighted in the glittering streak of mist at the foot of the pedestal—or was it a field with a sheet of plastic over it? No, it was actually the sea. The one giant cedar tree in the garden, deep-dark, bushy, covered with candle-shaped cones, was the façade of a grave-countenanced cathedral which, had it been offered us at eye level without our having to look up, would have impressed us as the natural goal of our journey.

But here where we had arrived we felt we had gone astray. The light was too much for us and its beauties were not only meaningless but offensive. The pillar-framed view from our arbor seemed a mockery. The vines blowing from shadow to sunlight wounded the soul. Never would we have dreamed that the birds of heaven—except, perhaps, for crows—could have become repugnant to us; but now we heard the same mocking screams from each of the many varieties in the cedar bower, and when the wood pigeons fluttered in place as though about to land on empty air, their slender throats had swollen to bull necks.

There was also our sense of guilt. Everywhere people were doing something, working or studying—here in the park, for instance, the gardeners with their apprentices; and down in the city those masons who had been working for years, faithfully rebuilding the cathedral with the original stones. What better occupation could there be in this day and age? And weren't those men, without being in a hurry, more than usually absorbed in their work? The lamb on the façade was already looking over its shoulder into space. The relief of the dove faced the morning sun with falcon's eyes. The three stone kings in their niches, all deep in blissful sleep, were once again following the star in their dream. Only the tip of the steeple still lay where it had been hurled, far away, in the midst of a thicket that had grown up around it. To us idle onlookers on the terrace, who had only to turn our heads to be served like kings, the repeated piping of the cash register in the background sounded like the distress signal of a rudderless space capsule that was carrying us away from our earth. So this was what came of trying to get rid of history, individual as well as universal, and escaping into so-called geography?

* * *

We were terribly at odds, and there was nothing to pull us together again. If the old man had reappeared and made a proposal to all of us, we would have laughed, not only at his proposal, but at his person as well.

Finally, after an hour or a month of silence, the youngest among us, hardly more than a child—the soldier—began to speak. Before he had even uttered the first word, his Adam's apple gave a violent jerk, the veins in his throat and forehead swelled, and he pressed his fist against his mouth. When he took it away, the whole lower half of his face was darkened as by a birthmark. When at last he began to speak, we saw no lip movements and might almost have looked around in bafflement, as if he had been a ventriloquist. His muscles tensed with exertion, literally making wrinkles in his clothes. He spoke softly but clearly, bent over his book as though reading from it, with the deliberateness of a stutterer who cannot be stopped once he has started speaking fluently. Like everything he did, his speaking was involuntary and unpremeditated; also quite casual, a kind of soliloquy, halfway between speech and silence. Was he, alone of us three, in command of that calm impersonal voice with which, even amid the confusion of innumerable other voices, a man can encourage himself? And yet under his crew-cut hair there glowered a darkness as of some suffering that demanded to erupt. All the time he was talking he passed what was left of the cave stones, along with the buttons he had ripped off during our journey, from hand to hand, and kept jumping up from his seat.

"Maybe my departed made false promises to the world. He entered into a pact and didn't abide by it. He called himself a suitor, but found no words in which to press his suit. He lifted me out of my depths and dropped me all the lower. He promised me a great country, and here I am alone in it among enemies. He made me think that the barren wilderness would be my fruitful orchard just because he had given it form. He was a false prince; he lured me away from home, from the barracks, from my people, to a country where there is not a breath of air, except perhaps for him. He was not a prince of a world empire for all; he was an illusionist; he made me betray my native village, he turned me into a deserter. My supposed prince turned my head, tore me out of my natural surroundings, brought me face to face with the void. And even as my scout, he deceived me. He had seen all sorts of places, but hadn't stayed in any of them. He was not a geographer, because he hadn't enough patience to bear witness as a historian. All he cared about was reading traces here and there, instead of writing the story of a famine, for instance, or of the building of a motor highway or merely some railroad worker's lopsided garden. As a result, he didn't guide me straight into the distance but led me around in a circle with his magic signs, deeper and deeper into a labyrinth. And just as he was a false prince in the open, he was a false scout in the labyrinth; for as a scout he should have been surefooted, should have found his way in country where he had never been before; with his steps alone he should have been the trailblazer.

"But last night I had these dreams: the first was about this book. It was ten times bigger and thicker than in reality, a folio volume. And I had a child that I carried around with me, hidden in the hollowed-out folio. But when I came to a safe corner and looked, the child wasn't there anymore;

it had disappeared along with its cave, my thick India-paper folio. After that I only dreamed words and spelled them out at the same time: 'How quick you have been to betray your childhood. That old man was not wicked, he was only an eternal child. The substance of childhood must not be misused.' My last dream concerned the future, and the sentences that went with it were in the future tense: We shall look for the man who has vanished. The search will take a whole year, and we shall search separately. You, woman, will remain here and wait; you, gambler, will drive your car from city to city, each day a different city—and I, soldier, starting from here, shall walk in wider and wider circles through the open country. We shall communicate every evening by phoning the hotel. Because the searching and waiting will slow us down and sharpen our senses, they will have a quality of always imminent finding. In the late spring, in drizzling rain, you will discover the old man's footprints on a dirty pedestrian crossing. At the summer solstice you on your terrace will see wheels of fire crisscrossing over the highlands all night long. After an autumn storm has died away I, in a dream, shall literally *pluck* the one scrub oak still growing on a heath and bring it to you as evidence. At the onset of winter, we shall meet in the seaport town at the end of a railroad track; the buffer will be the last hurdle before a dune and the sea. The station platform will be surfaced with tar, and stamped into it we shall find tickets, matches, and newspaper clippings, forming a trail leading to the dune. There in the tall grass beside a chain-link fence, the old man's notebook will be lying open, visible from a distance, seemingly unharmed. But the entries will have been bleached and blurred by the year under the open sky, and the pencil will be weather-worn. Nevertheless, it will write and we shall be able to trace the lines that have been printed on the paper. Even if only individual, disconnected words and outlines with no great significance come to light, the deciphering in itself, our bending over the notebook together, will be the most exciting, most magnificent adventure of the present era; and when at last we look up, the dune—I'm quoting my dream word for word—will be *our brother's tomb, glittering far and wide*. I refuse to be talked out of my old man. We must not let ourselves be talked out of our old man. His rediscovered writing has *flowered* in my dream."

At the end the soldier spun around in a circle like a hammer thrower, but then he sat down again as though nothing had happened. He covered his eyes with his hands. Bent forward, the woman thrust her hands between her knees. The gambler picked the pebbles out of the grooves in the soles of his shoes. Without looking at one another's faces, we were conscious of cheek lines and eye colors, and the three of us formed three couples. Around us all manner of sounds were swallowed up by the dead silence, as though the din of the earthquake were still at work a dozen years later. We sat on the terrace as at the scene of an air crash, each looking in a different direction and into a different space. In the middle of the lawn a stalk of prairie grass trembled when grazed by a bird. At the edge of the bower an ivy leaf beckoned . . . As we sat there motionless, a waiter put up a sunshade over us; leaves rained from its folds and some of them here and there sprang open on the ground. The drops on the glasses began for a moment to run. Wasn't the brimstone butterfly that suddenly flew past us a harbinger of spring? But the lone apple tree was bowed down with autumn fruit, which in time, under the influence of our heartbeat, began to swing like the seedpods of a plane tree.

A plane tree actually appeared—felled, cut up, and stacked into a long, splotchy woodpile. Had our water-drawing fairy-tale tree been chopped up? Had its twining branches been sawed into short, straight logs? The soldier spun one of his cave pebbles on the stone table; there was a notch in it which in spinning became a spiral, and when motionless was a crack.

Now at least we were something; at least we were un-happy.

In our grief we acquired the eyes of all human races. As though that gave us a kind of energy, the stump of the plane tree, which the gardener had left in the ground for the time being, emerged from still another direction. The uncovered roots seemed at one point to have grown together to form a hollow, full to the brim with rain or sprinkler water, whose surface quivered slightly. It was shaped like a human ear, and instead of swallowing up sounds it inten-sified them. The distant thunder of squadrons of airplanes and the howling of serried racing cars—and, intermittently, clear and penetrating, a child's voice counting slowly and concluding with the words: "I'm coming."

A jolt passed through all of us at once when we remem-bered how in childhood we had often hidden from others because we wanted them to look for us. A wind arose as though from within us, and permeated all things: the wind of poetry, the wind of fantasy, the wind of arrival in a very different absence. The park smelled of new-mown hay, and

the birds in the cedar tree called as though from field furrows. The bell in the cathedral tower, a motionless black
silhouette, hung. The straight stone staircases mounted.
The sunshades arched. The chambermaid leaned. We sat.
The gardeners stood. The walls stood. The branches of the
cedar tree crisscrossed. The roots extended. The magma
blazed. The sea surged. The cosmos whirred. The birds in
the sky glided wing to wing. The leaves greened. The tree
trunk grew rounder. The smoke gave signals.

I could write a whole book about our quest. But first
we were granted a brief respite. The soldier stretched his
legs; the gambler divided up his money; the woman put on
makeup and smiled at someone around the corner. In the
end we put our arms around one another's shoulders. And
for a little while all three of us just sat there showing ourselves.

Man's life between heaven and earth is like a white colt dropping into a crevasse and suddenly disappearing . . . Suppose we try to roam about in the palace of Nowhere, where all things are one.

CHUANG TZU